FIREWORKS

& Fertility

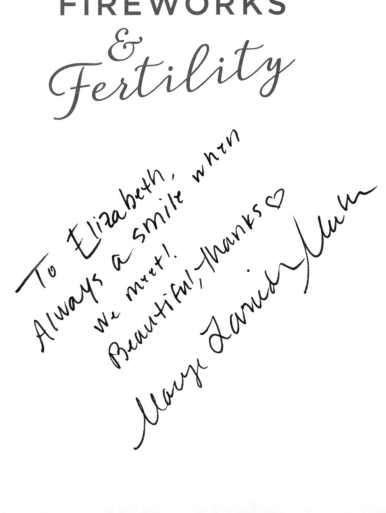

To Elizabeth, when
Always a smile when
we meet!.
Beautiful, thanks ♡

Marye Lanier Mum

MACYE LAVINDER MAHER

FIREWORKS

&Fertility

A NOVEL

GREENLEAF
BOOK GROUP PRESS

Published by Greenleaf Book Group Press
Austin, Texas
www.gbgpress.com

Distributed by Greenleaf Book Group

For ordering information or special discounts for bulk purchases, please contact Greenleaf Book Group at PO Box 91869, Austin, TX 78709, 512.891.6100.

Design and composition by Greenleaf Book Group
Cover design by Greenleaf Book Group
MrVander, 2017. Used under license from Shutterstock.com
©iStockphoto.com/McXas

Cataloging-in-Publication data is available.

Print ISBN: 978-1-62634-375-7

eBook ISBN: 978-1-62634-376-4

Part of the Tree Neutral® program, which offsets the number of trees consumed in the production and printing of this book by taking proactive steps, such as planting trees in direct proportion to the number of trees used: www.treeneutral.com

TreeNeutral

Printed in the United States of America on acid-free paper
16 17 18 19 20 21   10 9 8 7 6 5 4 3 2 1
First Edition

For Roy C. Kinsey, Junior
Thank you for building the Mill Mountain Star

For Alex, Beckett, Harper, and Leisel
Your unconditional support runs through these pages

One

GAZING PAST THE microscope to gather my thoughts, I caught my eyes in the reflection of the window. Chicago was out there, but I couldn't really see much beyond my face, the skin below my eyes, shouting "puffy." As the hours at the clinic soared, the sleep deprivation of a professional embryologist crept in.

The lineup for the day included thawing for frozen cycles, grading one more set of embryos, consulting patients, and, of course, the transfers, the replacement into the uterus of carefully fertilized sperm and eggs. I picked out the best embryos for a transfer procedure I'd do in the late afternoon.

I'd almost finished fertilizing the eggs from this morning's retrieval, a process called ICSI. It stood for Intracytoplasmic Sperm Injection.

Fanny entered the lab.

"I called you back, you know?" she said.

"Just a second, let me finish." I breathed in slowly, without looking up from the microscope. Using the operating handles, I held the egg in place and the needle to the sperm. I then injected the sperm into the egg. I exhaled and let go of the joysticks.

Fanny was watching me with one hand on her hip, the sign of mild agitation, which I knew would increase with our conversation.

As I walked the petri dishes to the incubator, I framed my thoughts. She had a muscular build and a symmetrical face with no freckles or blemishes. Her hair was the-same-all-over natural blonde, which surely made women who paid for a similar look envious. Her eyes were bold sky blue and could hold icy expressions, especially when the scheduling wasn't to her liking. We had little time out of the lab, so I was familiar with her glares.

"Did you want to see me about my schedule?" she said. "I'm just asking for my birthday off."

Hearing the click of the incubator door as it suctioned closed, I folded my arms across my chest. "No, one of our patients mentioned your sense of humor. Not in a funny way—said she thought you'd joined the field to get rich selling unfertilized ova on the black market." I held up a hand to stop her.

Her face pinched tighter.

"Our patients are under tremendous stress. You know that. If they had any question over the security of the eggs or the sperm or, heaven forbid, the embryos—"

"I would never do it. I was only joking." Her other hand had worked its way up to her other hip.

"What patient did you say this to?"

"You know, or you wouldn't be asking."

I smiled wryly. "Maybe you've said it more than once, to lots of our patients." I suspected she ran the joke amply. "Happens one more time then it's serious, which means consequences."

"Okay, I won't make any more jokes."

"Let Maple know I said you could have your birthday off," I said. "That is all."

She walked out. I wanted to hurt something. I had to be productive instead.

An idea flashed in mind, the recurring pop-up; my brainchild. I wanted to cultivate a place where women could relax and face the IVF treatment in a comfortable setting away from their busy, stressful lives. It was time to share the idea with my boss, Dr. Jim Masonrod. I checked his office, but he wasn't there. I found lanky Demetri instead.

In one hand he held a couple of typed pages. He looked at me nervously and then shifted his bloodshot eyes to the floor.

"You heading back to the lab?" I said. "I'll walk with you."

"Yeah, there are a few things I've got to finish up."

"Finish up?" The way he said it confirmed my suspicions. He'd only been on the job two years, the same as Fanny.

He stopped and turned to me. "Here's your copy of my resignation letter. I've got to stop working here. My wife is upset because I'm always stressed out. Says it's not good for me."

"Demetri, I never knew that's how you felt." Totally false—we all felt it. But it was part of the deal. I let out a heavy sigh.

"I'm sorry. Truth is, I think I want to be a vet or maybe a teacher."

"No, no, I get it. It's extremely intense just walking across the lab floor, holding a dish of embryos. All of the demands together—it's exhausting."

"Can you give this to Jim?" Dr. Masonrod insisted his employees call him Jim and his patients call him Doctor.

"Sure." I took the letters. I watched him walk down the hall, and then my eyes rolled into my head. My beeper went off. It was Daryl, the least levelheaded of the six embryologists—slash that—five embryologists I supervised.

She picked up on the first ring. "Oh, my God, Julia. You won't believe what I've done. I made the wrong recommendation!"

I cradled the phone and kneaded my forehead. *You've got to be kidding me.* Usually Daryl went zany about what clothes to take on a trip, not her patient recommendations about what embryos to put back. "Tell me what happened."

After listening for two minutes, I told her that her instincts were right; she'd encouraged the couple to place one fair quality embryo through the transfer process. But in looking over the file, she reconsidered and decided two would be better. The couple would know soon. In the meantime Daryl would be a mess, thinking a second would boost the chances for a couple who had already gone through three in vitro fertilization procedures, what we call IVF.

"Just wait and see. You made a great recommendation."

"Oh, now I just don't know."

I scanned Demetri's resignation letter as I headed back to the lab, hardly listening to Daryl. I stayed on for five more minutes, wondering how Daryl would take the news of Demetri leaving. Would she make it through? I washed my hands and put on surgical gloves.

During the next half hour I prepped the embryos and assisted the IVF doctor with the catheter and the placement of the embryos in the uterine lining. When we finished, I stared down at the sweet lady in a hospital gown lying on the bed. Sharon was one of my favorites. "I hope you knock it out of the park."

"Thanks, I hope it will work."

Sharon's face was pale, though her smile was radiant. She had an attitude I admired. I pushed the lever to raise the back of the bed. She moved cautiously, as if she were worried that the embryo might slip out. It was her first IVF attempt.

"It's a ways in there," I said. "You're fine to get comfortable."

Her husband scooted out to get ice water. She'd complained of a dry mouth earlier.

"I know it's all new to you." I took her hand and squeezed it. "I'll have you in mind and say a blessing for you and Trey."

"Thank you." Sharon squeezed me back and then turned to the fertility doctor. "Dr. Carter and you, Julia, and everyone here, you've all been so kind to us. I can't thank you enough."

He smiled back. "Please call the clinic if you have questions. Don't be afraid to bug us."

Sharon nodded.

I pulled off the gloves and took the empty petri dishes to dispose of them. "We'll talk soon, Sharon. Good luck!"

Fanny lingered in the hallway. "D'you hear about Demetri?"

I nodded. "Word travels fast." I started down the hall. "We're fortunate to have had him, he's a great guy."

"You should feel the same about me." Fanny was following me.

"You're a great guy?" I quickened my pace.

Fanny's eyes slit. "Come on—lucky to have me."

I stopped. "Listen, it's not been the best day. Let's continue this conversation tomorrow, okay?"

"Fine by me." She turned and muttered something under her breath.

I'd have preferred a muzzle in my hand to the empty petri dishes.

Two

I REALIZED I was sitting at the bar in my lab coat. Johnny, behind the bar, watched me slip it off.

"Hey, I liked the look." Johnny is average height, though he sports huge biceps. His face is round, and he's got wide eyes. He's a sweetheart.

I laughed. "I'm having a rough one."

I'd pulled my hair too tight into a ponytail, so I slipped off the hair tie. My auburn curls sprung out all over the place. "What really gets to you is that I only order one thing when I come in."

He waved a hand. "Boring," he said and grinned. "But you like routine. It doesn't bother me."

"Yeah, my mom tells me that's how she knew I would never listen, that I'd be too feisty."

"And that's why you're in Chicago, far, far from your hometown."

I watched his bulging biceps.

"And at Reilly's, the pub of choice."

"Yeah, my usual Thursday haunt." Reilly's had been here a while, on Ontario, close to the Hard Rock.

Janie swept in. She raised an eyebrow at my lab coat on the bar while she tugged off her leather jacket. "Beth called. She can't make it this week."

"Yeah, I know. She texted me." Her daughter's cough had worsened, so Beth took her to an ear-nose-throat doctor. Probably bronchitis—that's never fun. "Poor Amelie. She gets it every year when school starts up. This year it's just a little late."

Janie sighed.

Johnny migrated off to other customers, and I watched him pop the handle just in time for the ale to stop at the rim.

Janie chewed on her lower lip. "How about we go on our trip to Barbados?"

"Or French Polynesia."

"You been there?"

I shook my head. "Nope, but one of these days we'll nail it down." We laughed.

I apologized for my overscheduled life.

"You're always busy." She gazed at me with her doe eyes. "But now my dream is coming true—a Shakespeare play!"

"It's one of the best, too. I love *A Midsummer Night's Dream*."

Back to chewing her lip. "Yeah, why the performance is in October I can't say."

Her stool knocked into mine as she shifted off to go to the ladies' room. I pulled out my phone and out of curiosity—because of Fanny and the black market comment—typed a few key words into the search bar.

Someone bombarded onto Janie's stool, startling me.

"This seat open?" he said.

In the one bright light shining from the bar I caught sight of his pants first: charcoal grey, close thread count, expensive. I looked up as if I were counting stars.

"Yeah, my friend Janie."

"All right." He moved down one.

I realized my lips were parted like a gawker. "Umm, thanks. She'll be right back." I forced myself to type more key words. I tried to recall Fanny's comment about selling ova, but instead I thought about those white, dazzling teeth I'd got a glimpse of when this handsome stranger said, "All right."

He glanced toward me.

Janie shot in between us. Her brunette curls bounced on her shoulders. "Hey, where'd you come from? I've never seen you here before." She struck up a conversation with the good-looking executive easily, and I heard him say it was his first time at Reilly's. He didn't live in Chicago.

"I'm Janie Baker," she reached out her hand, "nice to meet you. Where are you from?"

A loud crowd entered the bar, drowning out his voice, but I caught most of what Janie said: She had a flair for the dramatic, loved this city, and wanted to give every visitor to Chicago she met her grand tour. I'm sure she was especially interested in giving it to him. She sort of did right from her stool, starting from Millennium Park at Cloud Gate, the huge bean-shaped sculpture, through her favorite pieces at the Art Institute, to the old Sears Tower, where she'd once stood on a glass ledge above the city. I'd never made time to do it, probably because I thought it might be too scary.

"You'd love it," Janie exclaimed. She patted the stranger's hand.

Johnny and I exchanged looks. I chose to google "unfertilized ova black market." It didn't get me anywhere. I tried "selling unfertilized ova," and then clapped my hand over my mouth.

Janie turned. "What?"

I flashed my phone screen. "Want to peruse a study on unfertilized hamster eggs?"

Her mouth twisted. "Gross. There is nothing normal about your job, is there?"

Johnny poked his head over. "Need another Stoli?"

Janie's animation grew as she turned back to the guy.

"No thanks." I brushed the hair out of my eyes. "We are just about to plan a vacation." I paused to think. "You know, Janie and I have been talking about it every Thursday, hmm, since I can remember. One of these days she really will talk me into going somewhere like Sydney."

He wiped the counter in front of me. "Get me a ticket."

"I'll go with the new couple," I said sarcastically, looking at Janie and the new guy, but they were staring at me.

"Yes?" I asked.

"Nice glasses." The new guy cocked his head, and the light caught the vertical indentation centered on his chin. "Are you a doctor?"

I didn't answer. I noticed the stool beyond him was vacant.

"I'm Luke." He looked from Janie to me. "You're Julia." He cocked his head again. "Janie says you do endorphinology. What's that?"

"I don't know." I laughed. "What is it?"

Janie shrugged, and he looked confused.

I liked him staring at me, but I watched Janie flirt with him. For some reason, I felt like holding my cards to my chest. I also felt chilled. All throughout the bar, the walls were constructed of hard, sharp-edged stone. With Janie sitting there, I was not likely to pull off mysterious. "You want to know what I do?"

"Yes."

But was he looking bored? Insincere? I ignored him and fired off at Janie. "Seriously? You don't know what I do?"

She bobbed her head. "Yeah, sure I do."

"You're one of my best friends. It's called embryology." I flipped my lab coat over to find my wallet and keys. "Johnny, bring me the tab, please."

After he finished with Dirk, another local a few stools over, he came over. His smile looked guilty. "He took care of it," he said, pointing to Luke.

"One drink?" Janie pouted a bit. "Julia, you're a cheap date."

"See you later," I said. "I've got to get some rest and start fresh in the morning. Create some schedule with one, maybe two less employees." I waved a hand at Luke so as not to seem rude, but I felt it. My face colored, which just made the day that much worse. Way to go, Julia.

Janie hugged me tightly. With no competition now, she was more gregarious than ever. "Will you still come to the performance?" she said.

"Of course! I'm not mad. It's really just me feeling off after a weird day at work."

As I walked past him, I could smell his pine-scented aftershave. Before I was too far away, I turned and said, "Thanks for the drink."

He gazed at me over his right shoulder. "Any time."

I felt a twitch in my heart. When could we see each other? How often? Why would he want to see me?

"You always come on Thursdays?" he asked.

I nodded. "So? You don't live here."

"I'm here a lot. Maybe," he casually looked at the display of liquor beyond the bar top, then back at me, "I will see you next week."

"Will see me?"

"Could see you."

My purse handles had slipped into the crook of my arm. I pulled them back onto my shoulder.

He squinted at me. "Yes?"

"Sounds like a plan."

He chuckled. "If I have another guy with me, don't be alarmed. It's just my bodyguard. He wasn't feeling great tonight, but I'm glad I came anyway."

It was odd information I didn't know how to assimilate, so I smiled back. "See you then." Walking through the doorway onto the street, I pulled my phone out to text Janie, asking where Luke was from. Then I decided not to. She'd probably show it to him, and I was already uncomfortable since Janie had witnessed our talk.

The weekend went by in a blur; most of it I spent working. I was busy on the lab floor and slammed with phone calls to return, but, luckily, there were no incidents with Fanny.

While eating breakfast Monday, Janie texted that Harrison from her drama group had asked her out, which meant I wouldn't have to feel badly for pursuing our new friend. So I asked her where Luke lived and got a one-word text back: "Manhattan." Should've guessed. She also knew he'd gone to Stanford.

I set the granola bowl into the sink, filled it with water, and thumped off the faucet. I grabbed a warmer coat, turned off the iPod, and dabbed Moroccan oil into my palms to tousle the ends of my hair. I'd fallen for the wood-flower smell of the oil, and I kept a bottle of it near the door so I could use it right before leaving my apartment. After taking the elevator down, I emerged into a new day in the city.

Elm and Cedar run perpendicular to Michigan Avenue and the lake. They were located north of the John Hancock Observatory. Beth, my best friend, and I met for a cocktail once a month in the bar at the John Hancock, which usually had stellar views from its perch, but maybe not today. It was muggy and cloudy.

I passed the John Hancock and told the driver where I was headed on Elm. Beth's home was magnificently appointed, on the top floor of a high rise overlooking Lake Michigan.

When I reached the door to the apartment, Tommy was leaving. His job at his father's General Motors plant was a long commute, and he had to put in longer hours than anyone. He pecked me on the cheek. "Welcome to the Ramsays'," he said. I gave him a quick hug. "Because of us, Julia, you don't need your own kids anytime soon." His eyes twinkled.

"Precisely." I glanced about. "Where are they?" A rocking horse blocked my way, and I pushed it to the side of the foyer.

Tommy crinkled his brow. "Big tub."

"Amelie must have played with the dog's kibble again. I know your daughter likes to leave trails for Yeti."

"She left the dog out of it this time." The cocker spaniel rolled her eyes toward us from a khaki beanbag near the sofa in the living room. "Amelie was up early. She wanted purple cake for breakfast."

Tommy upturned his already marbled and calloused hands, and I saw the purplish color from the morning's baking. "Nice lilac," I said.

"Thanks. Amelie's a handful." Tommy smiled. "Beth has something to ask you." Without elaborating he turned and headed out the door. I knew he was taking the stairs; he despised elevators. I watched his stocky frame disappear, noticing a tiny bald spot I'd not seen before.

I slipped off my shoes and walked through the foyer, toward Yeti in the graphite-and-shell-colored living room. The dog was balled up, tracking me with her big eyes.

When I entered Beth and Tommy's sanctuary, a bedroom with a large fountain, I made a mental note to ask Beth if this new fountain was modeled after one in Siena. Beth had studied there. She used her inspirations from Italy to create waterfalls for young children and the elderly fighting cancer. She designed sculptures as small as a baby's hand for hospital rooms and as large as a horse for cancer facilities. There were a handful of the smaller ones positioned throughout their bedroom.

I could hear Tucker beyond: "But I like the taste of bathwater."

"Don't eat the bubbles either." Eight-year-old Amelie laughed in her sassy way—eyes closed, head sideways. Violet bathwater and bubbles covered them up to their little necks. Her hair, lathered by bubbles, was dark, like Beth's. The bubbles in Tucker's golden locks looked as if he'd gotten hold of hair gel.

When Amelie opened her eyes, I said, "I think you look like you're feeling better. There's color in those cheeks."

"Even more if I do this." She smeared purple bubbles all over her face.

Beth dried her hands and then hugged me.

"It must've been some kind of cake." I pushed up my sleeves. "Did you save any for me?"

They nodded.

I splashed the kids and tried not to turn purple myself. "Don't ever grow up, Tuck. Stay forever young."

He stuck out his tongue. Water dripped out the corners of his mouth.

"Tommy said you had a question for me." Beth's black slacks were a little bunched at the knees from kneeling by the tub; otherwise she looked polished in her suit. I knew her outfit meant she had client visits.

"This is a good time." She shrugged good-naturedly, turning to the tub. "Tucker, now."

"Will you be my godmother?" he asked.

"Do you know what it means?"

"You give me candy?"

Amelie smirked.

I laughed. "Yeah, at the very least."

Beth grabbed my hand. I squeezed her back.

"Please, Ju-Ju," Tucker said. "Please."

I caught my breath and said yes at the same time my phone on the countertop buzzed violently, nearly vibrating off the counter into the sink. "Just a sec, it's my boss."

It was a text message from Jim: "It's about your job. We have to talk."

Three

I DIDN'T GET a chance to try Amelie's purple cake. I took the train north to the clinic. Was Jim's message about Demetri? Fanny? The schedule? Patients?

When I came through the front door, at least a dozen faces looked up from newspapers or magazines. I saw a heavyset fellow drop his *Road & Track* magazine. Quietly he retrieved it. I wondered how many of them thought I was a patient too. The room remained grave as I hastened toward Maple, who caught my eye from the reception area.

Maple dabbled on weekends in horticulture. We benefited from her passion because she enlivened our lobby with sunflowers, tulips, paper whites, and Gerbera daisies. But the atrium took the cake. Mist from the special waterfall fed the rubber plants, evergreen ferns, and vibrant orchids.

I leaned on the counter. "Everything okay?"

She raised an eyebrow and shrugged. "Seems that way to me. A full waiting room is a good day."

The phone rang, and I headed into the atrium, where I daily enjoyed Beth's waterfall. It won the highest accolades when we'd gathered designs for the office renovation two years ago. The sound of the splashing water was a welcome distraction while I waited for the elevator.

As I stepped out of the elevator onto the fourth floor, I nearly ran into Jim.

"Sorry," we said at the same time.

"Julia, you're here. I can't wait to share the news with you."

I studied his upbeat gait as we walked toward his office. He was taller than me by almost a foot and had excellent posture. He wore thin-framed glasses over his crystal blue eyes and had hair and eyebrows the silver grey of a fox. He gazed at people as though he intended to listen to them. When he spoke, he chose his words carefully, and he spoke softer and clearer than most people.

I sat in the chair he offered across the mahogany desk from where he sat. For being excited to share the news, he took his time. He laced his fingers together and lowered his hands onto the blotter. It was riddled with notepaper that was covered with markings and notations.

I swallowed. "It's really good?" I couldn't help blurting out.

"Yes, and Julia, please don't show offense that I haven't mentioned this to you. The utmost discretion was involved to get to this point."

He was killing me.

"We're merging Chicago Live Births with four other clinics. The clinics were very deliberate choices. A hypercompetitive search, followed by negotiations, led to this dynamic conglomerate."

"I know *your* performance is astounding," I said. "And you wouldn't accept any group that wasn't first class. You must have done a lot of homework."

He laughed. "I interviewed the firms who conducted the interviews."

"Where are these clinics?"

"Paris, Dubai, the Philippines—"

"What?"

He cracked a smile. "Did I get you? No, I'm domestic for now. The premier clinic is the New York Embryonic Center, and there's San Diego Fertility Care, New Orleans Fertility Specialists, and Lone Star Reproductive Health."

"That's in Houston?"

Jim nodded. "Well, what do you think? Keeping this a secret has been hard."

My synapses were on rapid fire. "Sage Swan is head of New York Embryonic Center. We're going to be merging with Sage Swan?"

"Yes. And my dear colleague Sage now knows all about you, from me. And you will be the one to make the announcement because you are the new supervisor for the merged clinics. It's obviously a new role, but one I believe you are suited for. I will retain supervision of this clinic here."

I put my hands on the desk and then my head on my hands, gathering my thoughts. I pushed back up. "Are you serious?"

"Serious as IVF." Jim was radiating positive energy. It was off the charts.

Breathing in, I nearly choked. "I am honored." I coughed.

After an hour I had learned a lot more about the new conglomerate with its mega-research pentagon. He told me I was responsible for counseling subordinate staff, hiring, firing, meetings, publicity, policy decisions, and higher-level issues. One needed a flow chart to figure out what "subordinate staff" meant. I would be leading the five directors, one in each clinic. At some point I would be sent to leadership training with a consultant who trained CEOs of Fortune 500 companies.

Later, I checked up on the phone with Sharon and a few other patients, and I sat in on Daryl's new patient consult. All afternoon I floated in high spirits. I couldn't wait to tell Sam Stone, my friend from embryology school. Jim had arranged for me to make the announcement in an interview with a local news anchor. The piece would be broadcast live to a dozen of the largest metropolises.

That evening, I stayed late at the office to catch up. I updated my charts and sent email. I considered reviewing Fanny's patient charts, but I decided I'd do so when I was fresh. I returned them to the general cache. The silence in the offices reminded me of the soft atmosphere of the Smith Museum of Stained Glass Windows. I had to stop myself from tiptoeing.

I took the elevator to the second floor and pushed open the lab door. I smiled at the large incubators holding our precious cargo. The lab was as serene as the offices. Sealed. Safe.

On the train back to my place, I called Mom and Dad, but they must have already been sleeping. After leaving them a message to call me, I FaceTimed Sam.

"What's this about? You've never FaceTimed me." She was in her scrubs. Behind her stretched a vast research lab. Even through the screen delay and graininess, I could see she was a little irritated. "I'm working."

"I can tell. I just left."

She raised an eyebrow.

"Can you talk?"

"Sure, I guess." She took off her gloves. I saw her arm jerk and then saw the smack of the gloves hitting the plastic liner of the trashcan.

"I have incredible news. We're merging with New York Embryonic Center and three others. And I'll be working with Sage Swan."

Sam gasped. "Whoa! Five clinics. And Sage Swan?"

"It's true."

"You know he's a fertility expert."

"I agree." I watched her closely.

"Remember when we heard one of his plenary speeches at the conference in Virginia?"

"Yes."

"I'm about to pass out."

"I know."

She blew out her lips and ran a hand over the part in her silky marigold hair.

"Do you think I could come work with him, too?"

"It gets even better. With this insane research-opoly I might have a chance with my idea. At least it will be easier to research the viability of my plan for a new type of clinic." I heard whimsy in my voice.

Sam laughed. "You've had that in your head for so long." She stiffened and told me how busy I was going to be. "You have to focus."

"I know! But that's where you could come in. You know, help me with the first hiatus fertility clinic, where patients can check in and stay far from the worries of their everyday stresses."

"I can't believe this." She would not be derailed. "The merger is a ginormous deal." She stared hard at me. "I wish I could be you. Like, who gets this lucky?"

Lying in bed, I'd finally been able to turn off my thoughts. I was close to sleep when the shrill ring of my iPhone roused me. It was Janie.

By way of greeting she said, "I think I'm too needy."

I cleared my throat. "What do you mean *too needy?* But a call this late . . . well, that's borderline." I grabbed my glasses from the nightstand and switched on the lamp.

"I'm too needy for Harrison, I think. He hasn't called."

"Can't this wait 'til morning?"

"Aww, please listen. I need your help. I didn't tell you I hooked up with him on our first date, and now it's like he won't even look at me when we're rehearsing."

"But he's supposed to look at you. You're onstage together."

"I know. It doesn't help that he's Theseus, the Duke of Athens, and I'm supposed to marry him. Me, the Amazon queen." She laughed, but it sounded stilted. Silence for a beat. "He looks at me but doesn't see me. You know? There's a difference."

"Well, let me think. Declare your independence. Don't let it bother you."

"Is that what you do?"

"If you recall, I'm married to my job. There is this good-looking guy in the lab, David Lazel. But he's five years younger and a little too into himself."

"You hang with Johnny on occasion."

"Hey, that's a secret."

"Not to me it isn't."

"And we're not serious."

"Then why's it secret?" she demanded. "You're exasperating. And what about the new guy from Reilly's?"

"Oh, geez." I sighed. "Hey, one question. Did Luke give you his last name?"

"Hmm, Ashford or something like it. Ashland maybe. Why?"

I told her about the "anytime" comment.

"You think he'll show this Thursday?" I knew Janie. She was at the other end, chewing on her lower lip. "You want him to."

"We'll see. Talk tomorrow. Good night."

"Night."

I plugged my phone in and snuggled down into the king pillows. And then I was sinking onto a soft lemon-yellow couch at a New York Soho coffee shop. The chai I held was too hot to sip. Luke and Sage were seated across from me.

Four

THE NEXT AFTERNOON I consumed several handfuls of sweets from the candy dish in the lounge. Later, sitting in my office chair, I couldn't tell if my wildly beating heart came more from the sugar or the merger news. All day I ran across happy coworkers and bubbly patients. It was as if they, too, understood the magnitude of synergy about to happen among the clinics.

An email from Jim appeared, requesting my help in coining the name of the conglomerate. Tucking a pen behind my ear, I sat staring at my laptop and thinking.

An email from Belle Harting, one of my patients, came through inquiring if acupuncture was recommended for her situation. I picked up the phone and punched the number. Belle clicked on.

"Were you sleeping?" I asked.

"Nope. Do I sound like it?"

"Little bit. Are the meds making you sleepy?"

"Sometimes. They're strong. I won't lie—I put my feet up a lot."

I visualized Belle, who was taller than most women and had no use for heeled shoes, with her longs legs dangling over an ottoman. I also knew she'd put her endorphin-charged triathlon training and TRX classes on hold for a while.

"Acupuncture has been used over the centuries to treat infertility causes. You could benefit because it can actually improve ovarian and follicular function. It increases blood flow to your endometrium as well, which you might know helps to grow a thicker, richer lining." I sat up taller and peered out at the autumn rain.

"That all sounds good. I seriously think it could help. So when should I do it?"

"Anytime throughout the IVF cycle. And you ought to consider right before the transfer of embryos back to your body, the implantation. And we'll let you know how the embryos are harvesting and, based on whether it's a three- or five-day transfer, when you should schedule that session."

"Okay, thanks. Acupuncture would be something new for me."

"Do you have any other questions?" I knew it was her third IVF.

"Not right now."

"You've gotten this far. I'm available if you have more questions on acupuncture or anything else." The pen fell from behind my ear, and I bent forward to retrieve it. At the same time I heard someone enter. When I sat back I saw David Lazel. I blushed, remembering my conversation with Janie the night before. I held up a hand for him to wait.

"And one more thing, Belle—the pacing of acupuncture sessions throughout your IVF cycle, even twelve weeks post successful implantation, can be therapeutic."

"More is better?"

"Yes. Call if you need anything else. I'll send you an email this evening listing your meds, shots, and procedures."

After disconnecting I closed my inbox and turned my attention to my staff embryologist. David stood still until our eyes met. Then he did the rub and scratch move throughout his blond and brown beard, a little scruff for the twenty-something.

"I'm sure you'll explain the merger to the press, but can you fill me in?"

That surprised me. "What needs explaining?"

"Think about it. We were all heads-down working, and no one knew there were merger plans."

"Jim wanted to avoid distractions."

David tilted his head and squinted. "Mergers are like wild animals, you know? You got a promotion. I'm expendable." His hand shot back up to the beard stubble. I thought he might wear a path in it.

"Come here," I said.

When David walked around, I reopened my inbox and scrolled up. "See this email?"

While David read Jim's previous message, I focused on his clean musk scent. I blinked a few times to gain clarity. "See, it says we're actually taking on a dozen *more* staff embryologists."

David's smile broke. He stayed close. "Good, because I didn't want to have to get some bartending job."

"And don't be afraid to talk to Jim either. He's not scary. He wants you to succeed."

I waited out a pause. "You okay with that?"

"Sure," he said. "I just wanted to ask you." He stared at me.

I took the pen from behind my ear. "Jim's asking for me to come up with a name to incorporate the five clinics." I paused. "I could use your help."

I offered the pen. He jotted while I brainstormed. We filled a half page with groupings of names.

Out of chaos came order. We decided on Advanced Fertility National. The name avoided using the word "infertility," and we'd have the option of going global and easily changing the name to "Advanced Fertility International."

He lay the pen on the desk. "It's not glamorous by any means, but it works."

"It's my favorite." Our smiles connected us. "Thanks!"

He stood and stretched. "I should get back to the lab."

I watched him walk toward my office door.

He turned. "You know the speaker in the lab making all the static? I fixed it for you. I know you like Sinatra when you're grading embryos. I do too."

"That's very nice, David. Thank you."

I called Jim and told him the name David and I had come up with. "That's fast work, Julia." I gave some credit to David. Poor guy thought the merger meant slashing the embryologists. I remembered I'd been nervous too, when I first received Jim's text. I laughed.

"What's so funny?" asked Jim.

"I was thinking how we're all so afraid of change."

On Thursdays we have staff meetings in the lounge at the end of the hallway on the fourth floor. I stuck to that tradition even though I had the live interview right after. I knew people were worried about the coming changes, so I wanted to maintain some sense of consistency.

Before the meeting, I'd discovered on the Internet a great deal about the man I met the previous week at Reilly's. Turned out his last name was Ashton, not Ashland or Ashford.

He was the head of Summit Enterprises, an international trading and holding company, and made deals around the world. The latest deal in the news had been for over a billion dollars, with a new ETF for Golden South Sea Pearls, which had previously not been traded by retail investors. My head was spinning. Would this jet-setting guy actually show up at the bar later, looking for me?

"Is Jim coming?" Daryl asked at the beginning of our staff meeting.

"Not today." I set my phone on the table. "He's working on the merger."

I looked around the lounge. Without Demetri, there were five embryologists: the sisters—Tia and Susanna—Daryl, David, and Fanny, who was unusually quiet.

We discussed patients and workload, and I read aloud a message from Jim about scheduling clinic visits. "He would like for one of you to join me in each of the cities."

Everyone started speaking at once. Fanny insisted on Manhattan. Daryl chose New Orleans.

Fanny clapped her hands. "Daryl, good choice for you because the shopping on Canal Street is fabulous. Hit it. And you know the food is out of sight, too. There's like ten great spots in the French Quarter." Her bright blue eyes clouded, diffusing her enthusiasm. She stopped talking abruptly.

I noted their preferences. "I'll give the list to Maple, and she'll research flights. If no one has anything else then we're done for today. For tomorrow, good luck with your embryos. Think positively."

Daryl's eyes twinkled. "Positive pregnancies here we come," she said as she stood.

"Charge!" we all said in unison. It was the way we wrapped every staff meeting.

There were goodbyes from everyone except David. He crossed his arms and said, "There's something we should talk about."

My nerves jumped. "I'm not usually in such a hurry"—I glanced at my watch—"but I have to be on camera in thirty."

He waved a hand. "No problem. What I have to say can wait."

He followed me down the hallway and into the elevator. I was surprised when he got out on the second floor with me.

I walked over to greet Jim, and so did David.

Later, deep in conversation with Jim about success rates, I heard David's rich, metallic-sounding voice as he chatted with one of the men on the camera crew. When Jim took a call, David walked over to me.

"What're you doing after?"

I froze in the process of pulling out a lipstick from my purse. The way he gazed intensely at me, I thought he was inviting me out. "Meeting a friend." I wanted to shout: "Are you trying to distract me? What are you doing?" I quickly grazed the lipstick across my lips.

He slipped his hands into the pockets of his slim cargo pants.

"Who?" he asked.

"Excuse me?"

"Who're you meeting?" He rocked on his heels.

"It's Luke Ashton." I blinked a few times. Though David was a lab rat, he might follow the news and recognize the name.

"From the South Sea deal?"

My head bobbing, I said, "That's the one."

"I know him. Yep, he went to business school with my older brother."

I cleared my throat. "Well, what a small world. Listen, I better move over to the ready position." I walked around him.

"You know how I really know him?" David asked.

I couldn't resist. I had the feeling he was about to tell me something I didn't know about Luke. "How?"

"Blackwater. I never worked there but learned that Luke did."

The name took me aback. Blackwater? The privately held security service provider? The face of non-government-sanctioned warfare?

"What does Blackwater have to do with Luke?"

"An aviation division needs a financial analyst. The sharpest, perhaps."

He shrugged and smiled at the same time, which infuriated me.

"I'd like to learn more, but I'm on."

The news crew sat me in one of two chairs they'd placed in the lab. A couple of microscopes on the counter behind the chairs served as the backdrop.

I felt David's eager eyes following everything I did.

Jim clicked off his phone.

David moved to the back of the room. Out of the corner of my eye, I witnessed him lifting a champagne bottle and appraising it.

Someone from the film crew clipped a tiny microphone to my blouse. I took a deep breath as Mr. Rosenberg, the news anchor, took his seat on the chair opposite me.

"Don't worry," he said. "It's painless if you act like yourself."

"Okay." Was my face as red as my hair? I reckoned it was.

"Clap while counting to six for me. It syncs the cameras."

"One-two-three-four-five-six," I clapped.

"Good. Hello, I'm here live at Chicago *Live* Births," Anchor Rosenberg said. "Before me is Julia Holland, lead embryologist and supervisor of the new conglomerate."

I painted on a grand smile.

"Julia, can you tell us about this merger everyone is talking about?"

"Yes, there's fertility synergy and energy in going big. Dr. Jim Masonrod worked on elite clinics with unparalleled success rates, higher than sixty percent for patients under thirty-five, to join in the mission of advanced fertility. With this traction we hope to use historical data and research-based algorithms to take us to seventy percent. We will improve the industry and advance the technology. This is good news for the people who want to start a family and have had difficulty doing so. We will be easily accessed in New York, Chicago, San Diego, New Orleans, and Houston, which will make our accessibility for international patients more convenient as well."

"Will this put other clinics out of business? Or will you work with them?"

"We want to share. The field is vast."

"What do you want to say to anyone who thinks this is a type of monopoly on the infertility business?"

"We're here to stay. We're here to deliver. All that being said— now more than ever—we have a lot of work to do."

"Earlier I had a chance to speak with Doctor Jim Masonrod, head of Chicago Live Births. He said a champagne toast is in order."

I said, "Follow me, then."

We quickly moved the interview and the cameraman trailed us out of the lab and into the hallway. Behind me there were pictures of babies and painted colorful images of embryos.

Pop! The cork bounced off the ceiling. The camera panned to Jim, happy in his element.

Grinning and holding a champagne flute, David Lazel stood next to him.

When I arrived at Reilly's, I found Beth at the bar.

"How was work?" she said.

"The interview went well, I think." I couldn't help glancing around the bar to see if Luke had arrived before me.

"Julia," she said and smiled and arched her eyebrows suspiciously, "why are you looking all smiley and starry? It's kind of creepy."

"Sorry, does it offend you?"

"Kind of." She laughed. "Did Maroon 5 call?"

"Better." After I described Luke we both looked to the front of the pub. Johnny saw us. "Guess you're looking for Wall Street?"

I met his gaze briefly, then watched him working a lager glass, twisting a white drying towel around and around the rim.

"What's going on?" Beth looked back and forth. "Are you jealous, Johnny?"

"Beth!" I sat back.

"Just wondering why she gets the cashews while the rest of us are stuck with the same old peanuts."

I enjoyed watching movies with Johnny, but nothing had ever materialized between us.

"I don't have a clue about you two." Silence crept up, until Johnny got a call for a drink at the end of the bar. Down the line of the shiny mahogany counter, I could see fingers drumming on a coaster.

"Hey," Beth brightened. "I have good news."

"Is it about a trip?"

"Way easier. I bought concert tickets for you, me, and Janie to see the Dave Matthews Band. It's the last concert at Tinley Amphitheater for the season."

"Are you for real?"

"We'll have to bundle up."

"I don't care!"

"What'd I miss?"

I could tell without turning around that it was Luke. My heart skip-hammered.

He pulled me off the stool into a cratering hug. When I opened my eyes I startled. I was face to face with a guy standing behind Luke. He had deep coal eyes. Looking into them was like staring straight down into a well. No, more like a mine.

"You're here," Luke said, stepping back. He looked surprised. "I can't believe it."

My sentiments exactly.

"Julia, this is Jason."

"Nice to meet you." I held out a hand. "And this is Beth."

"Come with me to a booth." Luke took our drinks.

With an agile move Jason slid in front of Luke. Although Luke was taller, Jason's broad shoulders were visible on either side of Luke's body.

Luke ordered a beer while Jason sat straight and tall and still. I knew Beth was trying not to stare at Luke.

"How'd you meet Luke?" Jason asked me, breaking the thaw.

"Here."

Jason mentioned that someone had called Luke twice and breathed heavily into the phone. They'd changed Luke's number. "Do you have his cell?"

"No, I don't," I said. "Can't take credit."

"Didn't sound like you anyway." Jason feigned relaxation.

"How do you know Luke?" I asked.

"I was a bodyguard for live pearls in the South Sea until Luke stole me away while he was working a deal in the area."

Luke listened to our conversation quietly.

"The ETF he created, only pearls instead of precious metals?" I challenged the bodyguard.

A loosening of the lips. "You can ask him more." He nodded toward Luke.

"Luke is a genius," Jason said, "He's not entirely unlike Mikimoto."

"I've heard of Mikimoto pearl jewelry. Tell me more."

"I have a few pieces," Beth exclaimed.

"Mikimoto impressively launched an entire industry single-handedly. Well, he had his wife, Ume. They dreamed of culturing pearls. That was a long time ago." Luke smiled. "I launched the revolution to let investors gain direct exposure to price fluctuations on the most precious kind of pearls. And"—he ran a hand through his wavy hair, and it fell back exactly the same—"pearls are easier to standardize prices on than diamonds. Diamond categories have many combinations of the four Cs—cut, clarity, color, and carats. Pearl prices are less intimidating. It just took me a while to standardize the pricing, but I had the good fortune of finding my bodyguard around the same time I discovered the premium pearls. From there we spent a good deal of time in Northern Australia and the Philippines with divers and scientists."

Luke motioned to Jason, who cracked a smile. "Mighty explanation, boss. But really, ladies, I find guarding people more dangerous than oysters. So, we'll see how it works out."

"I've heard it before." Luke tightened his eyes. "Jason likes to reserve the right to leave on a moment's notice. It's how he rolls. Or, how he was trained."

Jason kept his eyes alert and wide when he drank water, whereas Luke didn't even seem aware of his surroundings beyond our table as he worked on his beer.

I recalled the champagne cork pop from earlier. "So Jason wasn't here last week." I thought of David, the Blackwater reveal, that hadn't been mentioned so far.

"My travel path is top secret." Luke placed the drained glass by the edge of the table. "He wasn't feeling well, besides sometime I might mix it up."

"You're here two Thursdays in a row. That's not exactly clandestine."

"You're my type."

Jason laughed. Beth's jaw dropped.

My glass was almost to my lips when my phone rang. "Maple?" I said, my eyes on Luke.

Her voice sounded odd. "I came back to the office to check my schedule, and I saw David leaving with a box. Do you know anything about that? He's still in the parking lot. Do you want me to try to stop him?"

"Stop him from what? What kind of box is it?"

"Dunno. Metallic. Just looks strange, him leaving with a box I've never seen before. He's driving off now."

All eyes on me at the table amped my nerves. I excused myself.

"Can anyone just take embryos?" she asked.

"They shouldn't." My voice quaked. "Can you go check the incubators?"

"What would I be looking for?"

"You're right," I said. "You wouldn't know. You can leave, and I'll be there as soon as I can."

When I returned to the table, I apologized and told them I had to leave.

Luke stood up. "Really?"

I was so glad he didn't ask *why*.

"Are you okay?"

"Yes, I'm fine. It's just something for work."

Beth leaned on top of me while I reached for my coat. She hugged me. "Call me later."

"I will." I lowered my voice. "Sorry, Beth. This guy David at work is going to give me a heart attack."

"You're committed. Stay that way."

Luke walked me out. "If tonight's not going to go anywhere," he said softly, "how about tomorrow? I'll stay in Chicago."

My eyes met his. He was giving me a determined look—I think.

"You can do tomorrow night?" he asked.

"Yes."

"I'll come alone."

Catching a cab to Chicago Live Births, I pondered his closing: "Tonight's not going to go anywhere." Was he looking for someone? Someone like me?

Five

WHEN I REACHED CLB, I didn't bother with lights on the first floor. I found the red circle, buttoned the 2, and waited. The elevator whir made the whole thing even more surreal.

The lab room was quiet. Inside the incubator, though, embryos were harvesting, growing from one cell to hundreds of cells over the course of a fledgling five days. Or that was the goal.

I pulled open the door and took a quick inventory. Every shelf was full except the bottom one, everything just as it had been at six o'clock when I'd last been in the room.

What was I expecting? What did she think he was taking, patient records? Or frozen embryos? But that would have to be in a liquid nitrogen tank and not a box. What tripped up Maple?

Exhaustion swept through my body. I closed the door to the incubator. I just wanted to go home.

David was off the next day. I spent hours grading embryos. I reviewed Fanny's charts in the late afternoon, and I was happy to discover that there were no infractions.

On the way home by train, I took an earlier stop to pick up groceries for the weekend. I wanted the sun to shine and dry up this place, but it hadn't. I shifted my bags and stared at my feet walking across the cobblestone. As I got closer to Navy Pier, the neighborhood where I lived, I saw two little friends I'd gotten to know, siblings Rich and Penny.

Rich took a bag from me.

"Thanks. How was school today?"

"Ah, no fun. I had a math quiz and a science quiz."

"Really? Good for you."

They both looked up at me.

"What's so exciting about math? Or science?" Rich said.

"That's what I do for a living." I tilted my head. "But you have plenty of time to work out the things you love."

We reached my place, which was near Navy Pier. And Pier Park. And the IMAX Theater, Chicago Children's Museum, as well as the launching point for the best sightseeing boat cruises from the three thousand feet of pier on the shoreline of Lake Michigan.

The bellman took the bags from Rich and me. "Julia, I'll drop these for you at the top." He winked. It was no surprise I had to have the best view of Lake Michigan. I grew up by the water in the Keys. I loved the ephemeral changes in its bodies of ripple-wave-flatness. And I needed water for all the life forms of embryo and baby creation.

"Bye, guys." I hugged the children. "Have a good weekend."

"We're going to Pier Park with our dad. It's one of the last days for Wave Swinger." Penny wiped her bangs from her eyes. It was one of the rides at the park. The hanging swings rocketed around. I knew she loved it. "What're you doing?" she asked.

Placing my hands on her shoulders, I bent down to her level. "What you'll be doing in ten plus years. I'm going on a date."

As I revisited the brief parting conversation with Luke, I thought I might have the same problem Janie had with Harrison—wanting to stay over on the first date. I tried not to jump ahead while I dressed.

In the taxi to the Redhead Piano Bar—his choice—I scrolled through the images on my phone in the folder titled "Success Stories." I had more than five hundred photos of infants and toddlers, all of whom were at one time in the incubator at CLB. My plan was to print the photos and bind a book for Jim. The flood of babies from the merged clinics would be meaningful, but the memories of his first clinic would be unforgettable.

A kaleidoscope of vehicles slipped past. The cab pulled up to the curb halfway down Ontario Street. I recognized the maroon awning that led down a small staircase to the door, and I wondered why I'd never been in before. I paid the driver.

Was Luke willing to sing and be led along by a fanciful pianist? Or did he prefer an intimate table for two? Would he show?

I looked from one bouncer to the other. The first held his hand out. I dug in my wallet for my ID. This used to happen all the time, especially when I was out with Sam back when we were in school. When I first met Sam I thought she'd taken a wrong turn and ended up in the lab by accident. She belonged onstage. She exuded confidence. When we met, she said, "Wow, cool. A token redhead. I don't have one yet."

Because I always finished the lab exams first, she called me "Racy" for red racehorse. You know I didn't love it. We began sharing dinners and then studying together.

The bouncer turned the card back to me. "Have a good night."

A long bar across the room was filled elbow-to-elbow with patrons. My waitress reached me before I could unwind my wool scarf. She wore a face full of baby doll rouge.

"If you want a stool, grab it. When Dasher starts, the place fills fast. He'll be up any minute."

I ordered my cocktail and took the nearest stool by the curve of the grand piano. I studied the framed pictures on the wall of the father and son mayors. They looked to be singing as if they'd invented it, all happy and loose.

Luke appeared out of nowhere. "Hi, you."

Nervous and excited, I felt the pings of butterflies, the feeling I used to get before a tennis match when I was a high schooler.

I laughed. "You make me so nervous." Did I say that?

"My sentiments exactly."

I caught my breath. "I like the suit." I tugged a lapel and then yanked my hand away. I swallowed. "How did your dinner go?"

"Jason was smothering me, so I opted to let him get a work-out in."

"I saved a stool for you. According to the waitress, it's good real estate." My eyes darted about while I listened to Luke order a beer.

He placed his hands on mine, which were resting on my knees. A fire shot through me.

Dasher, the piano man, came out, and the stools filled up.

"I could just watch you." Luke's voice was calm and centered.

"You're welcome," I said.

"Huh?"

I felt like I was floating and must have sounded even more absent. "The stool. That's why you're welcome."

"Healthy competition."

Did he mean the guys all around me?

Dasher began to march on his keys. He had wide eyes, full cheeks, and wavy hair that bounced. We had a side view, an ideal spot to watch his fingers spring across the keys as if they were doing gymnastics. He sang, "Oh, baby—"

And Luke and I joined: "Well there's a light in—"

And everybody else: "Your eye that keeps shining."

It was an old Zeppelin tune, one of my dad's favorites. He'd listen to the cassette on an old beater tape player in the garage and sing along while he dickered with the engine on our first jet ski.

Dasher performed more eighties songs before taking a break, and before I knew it, Luke and I were sharing stories that involved family memories to songs by Eric Clapton and also "Sweet Caroline" and "We Didn't Start the Fire."

"I can't keep up with all the words. How do you do that?" Luke said and shrugged. "It's just not in my DNA." The waitress was passing, and Luke got her attention. "How often is this guy here?"

"Almost every Friday."

"Well, we have to come again"—he turned to me—"when I wrap up the next deal. It's in New Orleans."

"New Orleans?"

"Yes, why?"

"My new and improved career has travel benefits. I'm visiting the NOLA clinic in the next couple of weeks."

"I'm meeting my next shipment, it's coming by boat. My contracts are there because I have to receive them."

"Coming from where?"

His eyes twinkled.

"I won't ask more."

Dasher returned with Dave Matthews's "Satellite." I wished for Beth to be there; she'd love it. We sang along.

When Dasher finished up, I glanced at my watch.

"What's tomorrow look like?" Luke asked.

"Unfortunately, I have a long weekend of work. I have to be in early for frozen thaws and grading and prepping for procedures." I sighed.

He leaned over and brought me in for a kiss.

Six

"YOU KISSED HIM back and then you just stopped?" Janie was dressed in a medieval queen costume, her hair draping down like chocolate curtains. "Did you give him your number at least?"

"Sure, I did." The empty feeling in my stomach grew as I stared out from the stage at the three tiers—five hundred seats in all—of the empty Jentes Theater. We sat alone until a cast member dressed as a forest fairy came to gather her script. Janie asked her a few questions while my mind wandered to the embryos I'd graded over the weekend.

Janie's role alongside a good-looking troupe was so fitting for her that she might just get twisted up like the plot they were rehearsing.

I crossed my legs and watched the forest fairy walk away. "Harrison's attractive." It was an understatement.

"For once I have a shot with someone gorgeous. And I think I'm past the point of acting nutty around him. In the beginning I took your advice and turned him down twice. Then, he's begging me for dates." Her voice was fraught with yearning.

She laughed, and I was confused about how secure she was about it all.

"But the third date, the door was hardly closed and we were all over each other. I'll take him. I'm a green light. I'm an easy, easy—"

"Actress," I said.

She chewed on her lower lip now. "Why did you scram when Luke kissed you? Because of me and my lunatic ways?"

"I don't know. But hey, I'm happy for you. And I—I can't get too hooked," I sighed. "There's lots of travel ahead with work, and who knows if he's feeling what I'm feeling."

She pulled a loose thread, and it began to unravel the sleeve of the tulle gown. "Are you crazy?"

Save for the getting on and off of the other passengers and low rumbling, the train ride from home by Navy Pier to CLB passed in silence.

The train door swung open before I gathered my notes on patient profiles, but I managed to slip out just before the train doors slapped closed behind me.

I followed a couple through the front doors of the building.

Maple made introductions in the lobby. Violet Champion was younger than I expected, ballpark estimate thirty. Below her tawny, layered hair and chestnut eyes, she sported a shirt that read C'EST LA VIE, a short skirt, and black leggings that disappeared into cowboy boots.

After I gave a few instructions to Maple, Violet followed me toward the atrium, then through an arched opening. Three wooden doors entered into rooms painted different shades of green, with access to a fourth, the blood drawing room. The patient rooms had chenille rugs, love seats, and gauze drapes, along with sinks and a few obstetric instruments. We went into the middle room.

"Please." I gestured for her to make herself comfortable on the sofa.

She sat and dropped her checkered bag on the floor beside her feet. A book and a photo tumbled out.

Before I could begin, Violet started apologizing. "I'd just like to ask some questions."

I passed her the picture and book, *What to Expect When You're Expecting*. I sat upright on the swivel stool.

"My husband, Dylan," she held up the photo, "wants a baby like Neil Armstrong wanted to stand on the moon. Maybe more."

I smiled. "So what can I help you with? Are you here for IVF?"

"I didn't tell"—she paused—"your receptionist."

"Maple."

She nodded. "Yes, I was too nervous."

"It's normal to be nervous."

"I've used a clinic before. Twice actually. Dylan said I should try it again. I told him I needed to try something new."

"Tell me your concerns." I pulled out my iPad, hit the new screen icon, and entered her name.

"I was a patient at the Dream Fertility clinic." She slowly smoothed her skirt down and kept looking at the pattern. "I'm sure you've heard of it."

"I assume you were unhappy with the results," I said in what I thought was a kind tone.

Finally she looked back at me.

"Both times. The IVF doctor planned my schedule according to his because that's what they do over there." Violet slipped the book and the photo back into her bag. She crossed her legs, and clutched her kneecap. "We didn't plan on it taking this long to conceive. I mean, it got even longer waiting for my cycle to gel with the doctor's cycle. Oops—"

"I know what you meant."

As she described what she'd been through, the pitch of her voice flattened.

"I assure you that's not how we operate."

"What about holidays? Like if my Day 5 transfer falls on Christmas Day or something?" she asked.

"We are open every day."

Violet glanced at the door, as if a noise had caught her attention.

"You have a choice," I reminded her. "Certain doctors can be intimidating."

"Ridiculously intimidating." She relaxed her hand a bit on her knee. "I hope there aren't any like that here."

"I know it's hard to try again, a third time, but where there's a will there's a way. Also, our doctors are discreet, personable, and professional."

"I *will* try. For starters, I'll have my chart sent over from Dream Fertility."

I asked Violet's age. I had a sneaking suspicion she and her husband fell into that "under the age of thirty-five" group, where thirty percent of couples that came to us had no medical reason why they couldn't conceive naturally.

"I'm twenty-nine. Oh, I wanted to ask because I don't recall the prior details of both IVF procedures exactly. It would be helpful if we could go over them."

"Not a problem. We can do that, if you sign a form." I checked my watch. "I have time to cover how we handle IVF here."

After my final "bye" to Violet, I only had a few minutes to answer the messages Maple and Luke had left on my cell. Answering Maple was easy: "Jim said I should go to Houston first, so schedule that. Both Tia and Susanna will join me, so we'll need two rooms. The clinic is close to the zoo."

I delayed calling Luke since I was off to prep for the transfer of another patient.

The afternoon and the next day passed by in a whirl of procedures, and at night I hit the pillow, dropping into a free fall of sleep.

In one dream I met Sage. I was both excited and nervous about the trip to New York Embryonic Center.

Late Wednesday afternoon I remembered the metallic case that had sent Maple into a nervous tailspin. I decided to use an unexpected lull to investigate.

Descending to the basement where the lockers were located, I thought David and the others would be in the lab finishing up a process called ICSI, which involved injecting sperm into egg, scientifically engineering natural penetration. It was a good time to investigate since I'd have the place to myself.

"Anyone here?" I called.

No answer.

The basement held a locker room, a break room that no one ever spent time in since it was replaced by the lounge on the fourth floor, a sardine box of a room with an old elliptical trainer and a new treadmill, and a sitting room with a reclining leather chair. Every once in a while a male gave a sample inside this room. Other than that, it went unused.

The temperature inside the basement was as cold as a chef's fridge. Workout towels had been left on a bench, undoubtedly David's. An old lunch in front of a locker, likely Daryl's. And a well-worn yoga mat only halfway rolled up. That would be Fanny's.

I tilted my head back and was putting drops of saline in my eyes when I noticed David's locker. Curiosity rising, I moved toward it.

The door creaked as I pulled it open. "A-ha!" A metallic box sat at the bottom of the locker, a navy fleece vest wadded into a ball on top. It was a gun case.

Maple might not even know what a gun case looked like. And if she did, she'd likely never think that one of the embryologists would be carrying a gun, much less storing it at CLB. Blackwater came to mind, and now I was more curious than ever about how David knew about Luke, and if there was some kind of connection between the two of them.

I picked up the case. It was locked. It couldn't weigh more than eight or nine pounds. After placing the case back inside, I balled up the fleece as it was when I'd found it.

I took the elevator back up, determined to figure out why David had the gun and why he'd brought it to work.

Seven

FRIDAY, A MIRACLE happened: I left work by five.

Happily, Beth joined me at the train depot downtown. Tucker and Amelie were with Tommy. The potential babies at my work—the embryos—were hanging out together in incubator heaven. We could focus on the night ahead.

On the train I asked Beth about Janie. "You saw her yesterday? How's she feeling?"

How to label Janie's interest in Dave Matthews? Obsession? Lust? Wannabe rock star envy? So far, all three applied. I always laughed about the Dave Matthews coffee table books and that she had every one of his albums.

"She's still down. I didn't know whether I should leave her the ticket for a would-be souvenir or scalp it and use the cash to buy her schwag. It's burning a hole in my back pocket."

"Here, give it to me."

The seats on the train were filling fast as we rode toward the concert venue through a sketchy part of the city and then into the suburbs.

"Did you hear that?" Beth asked. She leaned toward me quickly. "Guy in that seat said there's been a shooting two miles from Tinley Park Amphitheater."

I drew in a breath. "I just want to hear some good music."

"Nice eye shadow," she said. "You're looking foxy."

I'd tripped outside myself and gone with a mix of plum and soft smoky grey.

"Thanks, but that's no consolation."

Our cab was waiting at the train station. We relented to a squad of four grungy students who managed to race from the train to the open door. I was fine with it, but Beth wanted to clunk skulls.

"We don't want to get shot," the only girl said. She had wide eyes like a tiger's.

At Tinley, the smells from the food vendors hit hard: hot dogs, pizza, and nachos. Beth zeroed in on pizza and got a slice for herself, while I got in line for Jack Daniels. I remembered the ticket.

"Anyone need a ticket?"

"Nope." "All set." "Give you five for it."

I hesitated. "That won't do. Sorry."

Beth found me as I was walking back to the opening of the amphitheater, juggling the drinks. The inflow of people began to thicken and I had to move sideways a few times to avoid an elbow or a shoulder.

To take a break from the crowd, I crossed to a brick wall and perched on the edge of it. I placed the ticket in between my crazy hair and the camo ball cap, something my dad had sent. I actually got some looks while I scanned the college-aged crowd.

Between eating her oozing pizza and wiping her mouth, Beth talked about the songs Dave might play. "It's a good seat," she said. "We're in the pavilion."

"Ticket for sale," I shouted.

A fellow and a girl stopped. They were holding hands. He wanted to buy the ticket because the seat was closer than the one he already had, but she didn't want to split up. Beth rolled her eyes.

Their heads both popped at the sound of a guitar riff. Even in the lowering light, I still wanted to get something for the ticket.

"Hey," a voice said.

"Hey." I turned toward it.

"I know you."

Know you? I stood up and my drink went sideways.

It was crazy and unexpected. Luke slipped a hand out, leaving me breathless, and he tipped it upright. When I looked into his eyes I somehow recovered.

"Need a ticket?"

"Yes, if it's near your seats."

"I bet you're here to see the band," Beth said sweetly. Using her charm, she re-righted the ship.

"Yes," he confirmed. "Jason's training a few guys in self defense, and I had a few calls to make. I slipped away when they went to the training facility."

Beth held up her empty paper plate and tilted her head. At first we both watched her scout for a trash can.

"The concert should be better than anything we've done," he said. "I mean, compared to Reilly's and the Redhead."

"It's perfect." I handed him the ticket. "It's yours. It was Janie's, but she'll understand."

Luke clicked his tongue and looked down as he dug in his pocket. "There's no way I ever thought I'd run into you selling a ticket. I bought one online." He examined his ticket. "It's not near your seat," he said, "so I'll sell mine instead."

I murmured that it was meant to be, while I watched him approach a teenaged boy.

"I didn't really think you could sell it that easily," I said when he returned.

"Here's your money back."

I stared down at the crisp one hundred dollar bill.

"Wait. What? I—"

"Interest," he said.

The longer I stared, the more his smile broke.

"You enjoy surprising me."

He laughed. "Yes, I do."

Beth cleared a path back to us. I gave the money to her.

I recalled Janie's words about Dave Matthews. "He floats in a different galaxy than the rest of us." I felt that way about Luke Ashton.

As we took our seats—first Beth, then me, then Luke—the show began with a series of drumbeats, followed by a sprightly guitar riff. All of a sudden more than a thousand voices belted out, "She wakes up in the morning" and "Ants Marching" was underway. On the expansive silver screen to the left of the band, a girl and a fox were running with each other, playing like they were friends. They ran in the garden among shadows, and flowers. Dave Matthews closed his eyes and tilted his head. His voice mesmerized me. The guitar and horns. I turned to Luke; his fist pumped the air with the drumbeats. "And all the little ants go marching."

"Amazing!" I shouted to Beth.

She took my hand. "I feel alive." Our fists vibrated together with adrenaline.

I'd barely unwound from Beth after that first song when Luke pulled me toward him. The look on his face told me everything was right.

Eight

"WHERE ARE TANYA'S embryos?" Fanny's voice over the phone suggested she'd already been preoccupied and overloaded with work.

Mondays at CLB were crazy. Whether embryologists worked or took the weekend off, there was always a flurry of activity seconds after arriving Monday mornings.

I wasn't there. Tia, Susanna, and I waited in the seemingly endless line at the rental car counter at Bush Intercontinental Airport in Houston. "Sorry?" I rubbed my eyes.

"Tanya's day-one embryos. I can't locate them."

"What are you talking about?" I knew who she was referring to—a patient named Tanya, who by reputation was a very intense attorney, maybe a corporate litigator. She worked hard. "Look in the incubator. Under T-B."

"Oh, I looked under the opposite, I guess. B-T. How did I do that? Got the letters backwards."

"No problem." I tried hard to keep the irritation from my voice.

"And are you ready for this? Two embryologists are here from Dream Fertility. Remember you promised sharing of information and blah, blah, blah."

"That's on the research end." I tried to keep an even tone, but both Tia and Susanna stopped and watched me, listening. "And later, after the merger, when the research pentagon has had a chance to get data compiled, analyzed, and reported—"

"Well, they are here now."

"Send them back. Say thanks, apologize."

"Okay." Fanny hung up. I'm sure she couldn't wait to send the Dream Team packing.

I unlaced my New Balance after a quick workout in the Marriott's exercise room. I showered, dressed, and was soon sitting in the passenger's seat of the rented sedan, giving Tia directions.

"Don't pass that car," Susanna said, leaning through the opening between the seats. "You have to get over."

Tia jammed the brakes, and the car screeched to a halt. Susanna whipped forward as far as I did. The light turned red.

"That's it," Susanna said, "next time I'm driving."

"It's been a long day," Tia grumbled. "Let's just get there."

Slightly annoyed, I glanced at my phone and scrolled down to Janie's text: "Call me right back." Tia was right, the two days at the Houston lab had been intense; we got to know everyone and their systems, and we shadowed them while they handled their procedures.

Tia was gunning it from zero to thirty to cross over to the far left lane to make a quick U-turn so we could head in the right direction. I deleted Janie's text when I meant to reply.

"I feel light-headed. I must be starving," wailed Tia. She gripped the wheel tightly.

"Okay, okay, there," I said.

Tia whipped a hard right. "That's a dance place. Like you know what I mean!"

Susanna said she was too tired.

I laughed. "At a glance, I bet the only girls going in are hired to dance."

The alley was tight, sharing a drive-up valet for both a nightclub and the Mexican restaurant renowned for the best fajitas north of the border. "Well, we're here."

Tia bolted from the car and tossed the tall valet attendant the keys. "Thanks!" she said over her shoulder.

Once inside the jubilant and colorful bar, I saw bartenders dispensing frozen drinks from machines, churning out orders.

"You mind getting us a table?" I asked over the din of Mariachi music. "I have to make a call."

Susanna and Tia both shrugged. "Sure," they said.

I went out to the alley. In the fading light the dance place looked really seedy but not threatening. The bench on the stone walk seemed ideal.

Janie answered on the first ring. "How was the concert?"

Her voice was so bubbly, I got on board. I leaned against the bench, a trickle of flowers hanging near my head. "You would've loved it. Really. They played 'Warehouse,' and I know you adore that one."

"Oh, God, you're so lucky." She coughed. "And Beth said Luke showed up."

"Indeed he did."

"You know I've been sick?" she said in a playful voice.

Quiet space.

"You're pregnant?"

"You of all people should've known."

"When did you find out?"

"About two hours ago. I went into the theater, and I looked for Harrison. I was shaking, but God, I didn't know what else to do."

Run.

"Harrison was there, by himself?"

"Yes. We had plans to meet and go over one of our scenes together."

"Is it possible Harrison asked you to marry him?"

"You don't know Harrison." Janie sounded skeptical and offended.

I batted the flowers away. "Sorry." I'd only met him once, when I dropped her for the audition, after she and I had stopped for coffee.

"He said we should keep the pregnancy a secret so I could stay in the play."

My mind raced. I wondered about his intentions. "It happens."

"Julia, I can't wait to have a baby."

"This is insane." I was at a loss for anything other than shock.

"We're going out tomorrow. And I think if I do what he says, I believe I can keep the part. But I have to be a really, really good actress if I get bad morning sickness."

"I'll keep my fingers crossed you don't." My astonishment faded. The play began the following weekend and would run through the first half of November. "Good luck. I don't want you to lose your dream."

"That's not happening."

Back in the restaurant, the hostess walked me to a weathered bench table where the sisters sat. The planks looked ancient enough to have been from a Spanish pirate ship. The sisters were sipping drinks as colorful as an Aztec blanket. My thirst kicked in.

"Those look good, and I'm starving," I said as I stepped over the bench. "I hope you ordered the fajita supremo."

"We did," they both said.

"Normally it takes months or longer to assess clinics. But looks to me like Jim did a fabulous job. What are your thoughts about the Lone Star clinic?"

Susanna set her drink down first. "I'm impressed. The place is immaculate." Her eyes sparkled. "Maybe we can learn something from them."

I recalled Jim's notes. "One of the first reproductive doctors from a premiere Los Angeles treatment center started Lone Star."

"Over thirty years of specializing?" Tia asked.

I nodded. "You said maybe we could learn something. Where are you going with that?"

Susanna tilted her chin, her flax hair falling into her eyes. "I'm thinking."

I waited.

"They score the inner cell mass and the trophoblast same as we do," Tia said, "so that's standard."

She was referring to a grading system created as a way of measuring quality across the board for embryo development over a period of days in the lab. I learned this early in my career and had used it since. The first grade (given a letter A, B, or C) assigned for the inner cell mass, which becomes the baby; the second grade (also given letters A, B, or C) for the trophoblast, which will become the placenta. AAs were the highest quality, and they had a better chance of succeeding after being transferred back into the female body.

Susanna scowled. "The biggest difference to me has to do with how they label embryo dishes. Lone Star uses social security numbers. The labeling at CLB has always been a thorn in my side."

"That came up at the beginning of the week with Fanny. She got confused."

"Yeah, but you also looked nervous." Susanna smoothed her hair back.

"Hard not to be. Ah, here we go." I cleared some room as the waitress stood by me, fajitas sizzling. She set the tray down, the three meats still cooking alongside onions and peppers. The tray rested on a rack a foot above the table. Another waitress clinked our glasses, shifting room for bowls of fresh salsa, cheeses, and homemade tortillas.

"Will you have another margarita? Daiquiri?" the waitress asked.

Picking up a fork, Tia nodded. Susanna too.

Tia narrowed her eyes. "You mentioned Fanny."

I nodded, in the middle of a mouthful.

"I don't think she's all that much trouble," Tia said. "David's the one you need to worry about."

I swallowed. Not having alluded to any issues with Fanny or David, I studied Tia's round face and the look of skepticism in her eyes, but I didn't ask more.

The next day was Thursday, and I was feeling behind on my work from CLB.

Needing a change of venue to check in with Jim, I opted to take a cab from the New Orleans airport to the French Quarter. Daryl could meet me there, and then together we could check into the hotel. Luke had business in New Orleans, and perhaps I could stay over Friday night as well.

I'd barely hit Café Du Monde when Luke rang my bell.

"Hey gorgeous, thank God you told me. I was thinking we'd meet up in Chicago but this works so much better for me. My jet was all ready."

Your jet? I took a seat under the green and white awning.

"Are you still there?"

"Yes, you surprised me."

"Oh, well, I can take the jet down in the morning. I always have work there."

What else was I missing about Luke? I reasoned these were interesting surprises. Remarkable even.

"It's fabulous." Slightly needy all of a sudden, I held the phone tighter. "Just before you called I was thinking I could stay here if you would be in New Orleans too."

"When do you have to get back to Chicago?"

"By Monday."

Three cabs snugged to the sidewalk, dropping passengers. Over a dozen tourists shimmied inside the wrought iron gate around the outdoor restaurant. French doughnuts for dinner.

"You sound different. What can I do to help?"

"Your coming here doesn't explain what you're doing in New Orleans," I teased.

"Running into you. Running a deal. Both."

I thought a moment.

"You're not saying anything again."

"I'm grinning, okay?" I flapped a hand through the air. If he was coming, did we need two hotel rooms? No one was watching me in this crowded place, but I still felt my face flaming.

"You can stay at Hotel Monteleone with me."

"And end up your—" *Worse things could happen.* Several beeps, an interruption, coming from Chicago Live Births.

He was laughing. "Fine time to have to leave our conversation. See you tomorrow."

I watched the large party working out the seating at two tables. The smell of sugar and fried goodness started a series of lurches in my stomach.

"Hello, Julia."

"Hi, Jim. Just getting settled in New Orleans. I was about to call you. What's going on there?" I took my wallet out of my purse and headed to the counter to make a decision while I talked.

"Good news. Dr. Carter's nurse called. She says Sharon's transfer was a success. Her blood level's looking good, so she's a positive pregnancy. We're continuing the usual meds. Sharon wanted to thank you personally."

"That means a lot. On her first try, that's just great. Doesn't get better." The counter girl thrust a menu my way. I covered the receiver and ordered three beignets.

The air felt thick and breezy, though warm.

"And one other positive. Your patient Belle has quality blasto-cysts this time. We're looking good for her transfer tomorrow; she'll be in for pre-op with a nurse this evening."

"Another ace. I wish I was there to help." I returned to my table. "Please make sure the acupuncture is set beforehand, if she still wishes."

"I'll tell Tia to tell her for you. Belle likes your bedside manner."

"That's kind. Did you have a chance to review Fanny's files? I'm trying to consistently check up on her."

"Bad news there." He stopped.

"So?"

"Fanny's file for Carrie Beaumont didn't match what the quality grade looks like when I checked."

"The new patient?"

Jim said, "Yes, that's right."

I leaned forward. "Son of a gun."

"Don't panic," he said.

A waiter delivered the square doughnuts dusted white with powdered sugar. My brain simmered as I stared at them. "How do we fix this problem?"

"Welcome to my world. I'll call the patient directly, switch embryologists for grading. I'll oversee the embryos from here out. You can deal with Fanny as soon as you get back."

I fast-forwarded to Monday. Serious consequences? This time, yes.

Nine

MARIA JOSE, THE senior embryologist at the New Orleans Fertility Specialists office, greeted me as I entered the lobby. Daryl, as usual, was punctual. She jumped up from the patient sitting area.

"How was your lunch?" Maria Jose was jovial. "It's always good around here."

Shopping bags indicated that Daryl had already done some damage at the Canal Street shops. The clinic's location was central, a block from both the St. Louis Cathedral and the river and not far from Canal Street.

"It's very good," I said.

I was telling her about the crawfish etouffee when I noticed Maria Jose tuck her hair back. Today's earrings were the biggest emeralds I'd ever seen. The setting was gold, the other feature diamonds.

"There's definitely strength in Creole," she said. "I have a great shrimp etouffee recipe, if you like shrimp. I could email it to you."

"Thank you." And Daryl agreed.

"Please follow me."

Maria Jose led us to her office in the new section of the clinic. Along the white corridor hung photos of barges on the great Mississippi. I listened as she told us about how her father, Martin, assisted in reshaping the river to improve passage around the three ports: New Orleans, Baton Rouge, and South Louisiana. "The South Louisiana port is one of the largest bulk cargo ports in the world. And when Katrina hit in oh-five, he nearly had to start all over again."

"I bet," I said. "Your family came up from Latin America?"

"Yes, my parents and two brothers. I was four. I don't remember much about Colombia."

Light came in from the southern window of Maria Jose's office, and my eye fell on a row of baby pictures on the long windowsill.

I raised both palms. "IVF babies from here?"

Maria Jose's eyes narrowed. "Can you believe this?" she said. "There were over a thousand frozen embryos rescued from a flooded and abandoned hospital. This was during Hurricane Katrina. The canisters, these massive metal things containing the embryos and liquid nitrogen, were discovered at a hospital. The Army and National Guard found some old flat-bottom boat to use. There was this deal about keeping the canisters sufficiently filled with liquid nitrogen so the embryos stayed in their frozen state."

"Of course, the tanks must stay filled or the embryos will defrost," I said. "Then what?"

"They somehow found the canisters on the third floor. They only had flashlights. They got them down to the flooded first floor, and the rescue team took them out to a boat. It's amazing. They were transferred to Metairie and then here."

Daryl took a moment to make the connection. "The babies in the frames are the rescued embryos."

The Gerber-looking crew ranged in shades of creamy skin tones, but they all had little bulb-shaped heads and huge smiles. I took out my iPhone. "Can you pose with them?"

Daryl moved to the side to allow Maria Jose to stand by the dozen faces. Her emeralds flashed, her teeth gleamed white through her wide smile. I leaned forward and clicked.

While I was sending the photo to Jim, Maria Jose's pager beeped. "Vamonos!" she said.

"What do I do?" wailed a stunned embryologist inside the lab room.

The other staff embryologist explained the problem: CO_2 and pH were off balance in one of the incubators.

The incubator is programmed specifically to optimize the embryo's growth environment. There's an inverse relationship between the CO_2 and pH levels in the incubators. Imbalance puts stress on the embryos as they are growing in the petri dishes inside the incubators. This New Orleans clinic used an older style infrared measurement device to balance CO_2 and pH. I'd seen it before.

Maria Jose stood confident, yet quiet.

I debated whether I should share my speculation.

"What do I do?" came the same question from the embryologist.

"If you can adjust CO_2 to get the pH in the range of 7.2 to 7.3 you will be fine," I explained.

"I know, but how can I tell if the meter reading is off?"

Given that I always traveled with the best device, I returned to Maria Jose's office and got the CARBOCAP handheld meter for them from my purse.

"You sure it's reliable?" A dubious look from the New Orleans embryologist.

Daryl stepped up. "We use one in the lab because it's the most accurate carbon dioxide sensor. I'll show you how to use it."

"Thanks, I'll be able to sleep tonight," said the embryologist.

Maria Jose brushed my elbow and whispered, "Me too. Think you can leave that with us?"

"Yes, I will. I'll have our administrator Maple get us another for travel."

"*Genial! Chevere!* You saved us."

"You're welcome."

"I know one person who's going be green with envy for my

shopping," Daryl said, "and give you a mouthful about handing off that CARBOCAP. And that's Fanny."

Maria Jose's hands shot to her hips.

I laughed. "Sorry, that's exactly what Fanny does."

"Who's Fanny?"

"A staff embryologist at CLB."

"But Fanny who?"

"McCloud."

"That's insane. I had to let go of her, Fanny McCloud. There could only be one."

"Let go? Fanny worked here?" I couldn't believe it.

"She was here eighteen months."

"Well?" Daryl said. "How did she get a job at CLB?"

Because she's a good liar? I raised my eyes to both Daryl and Maria Jose. "I don't know. I'll have to investigate."

"Can you tell me why you fired her?" I asked.

"I suspected she mixed up some of the Katrina embryos, but I have no evidence. I pray to the Lord above that she didn't. But I fired her on the grounds that she routinely skipped staff meetings and one transfer. We covered, obviously, but you can't have that."

Leaving the fertility clinic was like stepping from dry storage into a sauna. Daryl indicated she needed to catch a cab immediately or she'd miss the flight home. "Are you okay?"

"Here's a cab." I dropped my hand to my side when the cab rolled to my feet. She could read my mood and didn't ask again.

"Thanks." While the driver hauled her wheeled suitcase to the trunk, Daryl pushed the bags containing her luxury goods across the backseat and then crawled into the cab. She gave me an okay sign.

I held the door open to keep the driver from shooting into traffic. "You know to stay discreet about Fanny."

She gestured the same okay. I could see anxiety in her eyes. Noting her discomfort, I brushed her arm. "Daryl, thank you for coming."

"Pleasure's mine."

I knew she meant it.

The lights of New Orleans were glowing red all around me. I tried to call Luke from the cab as I watched the trinket shops and restaurants go by. The honking made me smile. It reminded me of home.

I stared at the "frozen" man on the cobblestone street corner near where the cab stopped at a stoplight. His face was painted blue with white stars, but his ears and bald head were not painted.

I wanted a closer look, but the window lever didn't work. "Can you please roll down my window all the way?"

"The Star-Spangled Banner" coming from a CD player built to its gusto finish.

"My friend Jaxeebo," the driver said. "Freaks me out—he can stay so still. See that."

Lateral red and white stripes were painted on his neck, disappearing beneath his shirt. The stripes reappeared on his forearms and wrists. He stood atop an upturned bucket. A smaller one stood by his anchor foot, for tips I guessed. I trained my eyes on him when we started up from a stop. "I like his cape."

Jaxeebo didn't move.

Two blocks later we pulled to the front of the Monteleone. "Ya here."

"Thank you. What's your name?" Leaning up, I heard him say "Hemingway."

"Like the author?"

"Like the author. But no 'G.' My ancestas took care a Mista Heminway whenever he stay dere. Kinda took to it, ya know?"

I thanked him, and accepted his calling card to be polite.

"I be at ya service, if ya desira."

Crisp blue flags flapping on the hotel's dormers caught my attention. I turned back to him. An Omega watch gleamed on the arm he draped over the seat. I showed him mine.

"Oh-meg-ah. Enjoy Nola, Miss. Here, let me get the door for ya."

I felt him looking after me. I turned. "Thank you, Heminway."

"Not forget to see the Caroosell Baw."

"I will. I mean, I won't. Have a good night."

He waved a big, muscular arm and then was gone.

Staring around the lobby, I thought I might see Luke. I asked at the front desk.

"You must be Julia?"

"Jeremiah" was embroidered on the receptionist's blouse, which was the same blue as the flags flying out front.

"Mr. Ashton is on the top floor. Penthouse suite. Please use the elevator in the corner by the Carousel. The main one doesn't access the roof."

Remarkable Luke, per the usual. I followed Jeremiah's directions. Fanny slipped from my mind, and I relaxed with the evening taking on a new course. Nothing could prepare me for the night ahead.

Ten

STEPPING FROM THE elevator, I saw a gorgeous outdoor swimming pool lit up from all angles. Flowers around the pool glistened, reminding me of my trip to Long Island in the Bahamas with my parents. Coral and pink blossoms offered up stamens that looked like fingers. I fled down the hallway toward Luke.

I heard the click of a door latch and turned.

Luke stepped into the massive doorway. I moved so quickly to him that we crashed into each other. He drew me back.

"You're pretty." He gazed at me.

"This isn't high school." I laughed nervously.

"Life should be this easy."

"What?" I asked.

"Never mind, come in." We entered through heavy wooden doors into a room with a high ceiling. The dark greens and golden hues of the décor accentuated the historic feel, and the vast living area smelled of an old library with the fragrance of flowers—lilies and roses—mixed in.

"The Carousel Bar's still pouring drinks," I said. My nerves were not gonna hold up.

"We'll do that first."

He placed my rolling suitcase up against a wall, and we left.

My heart pinged *mistake, stay here now*. It also welcomed a drink to help relax the inhibitions.

Side by side we entered the Carousel Bar. Heminway had it

right. When my eyes adjusted to the nearly white neon bulbs, I saw luxurious stools fronting the circular bar. Smooth jazzy sounds surrounded us, and I recalled one of my Karl Denson favorites. The air was humid and briny. I could also smell popcorn. Luke and I took the only open seats at the bar and ordered chilly apple martinis.

Holding the stem carefully, I raised the glass and waited.

"What do you think, Julia Holland?" Luke clinked his glass against mine. "The lights are streaming down on you like at the Dave Matthews show. The stage lights were all about you. How did they know you were in the audience? That's what I want to know."

"You can say that," I said, "but there's an awful lot of fool's gold in here." I gestured to the whole bar. "How do you know I'm the real thing? And how do I know you are too?"

Luke set down the drink. He released his grip.

People came and went to and from nearby seats, moving around us like we were a broken-down float in a Mardi Gras parade.

"How can I tell?" With one hand he took a strand of my curls and twisted it gently. "Or show you how? I have never known this. So now I know."

"I saved you more looking?" I asked.

"Let's just say, oh I don't know what to say. You're different. Every time I see you. You make me crazy. The freckles. The work comes first. The everything."

Interrupted by our tuxedoed friend, I watched Luke order another drink. Oh my. I shook my head.

Luke's phone rang.

"It's okay," I said. "Take it." I could feel the flush finally retreating from my face.

Luke muttered something and then punched to connect. He slid from his seat, positioned the phone, and shifted into work mode.

I pulled out my phone. The only message was from my mother. She'd found the snorkel and mask I'd had when I was six. They'd been in the very last box she'd searched. I wanted to give them to Tucker. They should be at my place by the time I returned home from New Orleans.

"What's on your mind?" Luke slid onto the barstool.

"And you're back." I reached out and pulled at his white shirt. He had a voracious expression in his eyes. I chalked it up to curiosity.

"A little boy." I tilted the drink and my head closer.

"Imagining me as a boy?" Eager.

"That's not it."

"Your first boyfriend." On the offense.

"Tucker Ramsay."

He chortled. "Sounds like a linebacker. He fell for your freckles across here."

At the same time Luke traced a path below one of my eyes to the bridge of my nose, the carousel bar beneath us began to spin.

Luke pulled back. "Why are you bringing up old boyfriends?"

"I'm not." The seats ringing the bar ebbed to a stationary position. "He's my godson. Beth's son. He's four."

"And?"

"My mom finally found my old snorkel and mask from when I was a kid. Beth has an enormous Jacuzzi tub, and I plan to give Tucker some shells and the snorkel and mask." Luke's eyes narrowed. "He can dive for the shells.

"Anyway, I hated baths when I was little; it was all Mom could do to get me to take a bath after being in the ocean. Sometimes she put in a starfish. And bubble bath to imitate a foam line. It worked. But I still kind of like the smell of the beach better. You know what I mean?"

Luke drained his drink. He looked at me. "I wouldn't know. I'm not a great swimmer. But let me tell you what I could do with you and a snorkel and mask."

"Could you elaborate?"

He did.

The penthouse lights glowed like stars above.

"Close your eyes," he said.

Maybe this was how Janie felt, too. Why wait when you're already at that exact moment you've been reaching for?

When I lay back on the white pillows of the bed, my eyes saw the underside of the lids, charcoal. All my other senses waited—on overload.

I had to keep from squirming as he unbuttoned my blouse with a light touch. It tickled. I bore it.

He placed a warmed towel under my neck. I sank into it. It felt like moist sand. "Where did you get this?"

"Spa delivery."

My lips seemed like they were stuck together. I pried; they opened. "How'd you know how good this feels?"

"Business school."

I laughed and opened my eyes. His short blond hair was finally spiky, not perfectly combed. "You've got to be kidding me."

He bent over me, and then used his teeth to separate my blouse. "That's all the talking for now." He kissed me from the navel up.

An hour later, I got up for water.

"May I help you?" He brushed a hand over my lower back. He dropped onto the white sheets.

"I'm coming back."

When I returned I studied him. "What was that call about?"

"When we were in the bar?" Lazy. But stalling.

"Something that's going to cause problems?" I felt the water chipping its way down my throat.

"No," Luke said. "It shouldn't. My latest deal is, say, in a place not known for niceties." His voice hardened. "I'm a little worried."

I blinked. "Go ahead. Where is it? Middle East."

Instead he pulled me down beside him. "What keeps *you* up at night?"

Brushing away my hair, I smiled. "I'm looking at him."

He scooped me up and slid me under him.

"I knew you wouldn't want to wait to find out the bad news." It was Jim, likely calling from CLB even though it was 2:11 in the morning. My brain couldn't work at that hour.

I slipped from bed so not to wake up Luke. "Hold on."

I'd never considered Jim a heavy breather until now. I stumbled through the darkness until I came to the bathroom door. I clapped my hands over my eyes when I switched on the interior light. I wanted the other light, the one that was more dim and manageable. I fell flat against the wall and sank down onto my heels. The marbled bathroom, large and airy, came into focus.

"Belle and Theodore?" he asked.

"Who? Oh, yes, yes."

Jim talked, and I listened. The entire thing seemed impossible.

Eleven

MY PHONE STUCK like a magnet to the side of my face. My whole being was rigid with fear.

"During Belle's transfer we placed a blastocyst with a quality of a double A into her uterine lining to implant."

By our standards, this was the highest grade for both inner cell mass and its trophoblast. By our measures, this was the best she could have. I stared at the marble.

"I'm telling you the embryo is not Belle's; it belongs to someone else."

My stomach tightened. "Hers were good," I said, "but not perfect, not double A. You think it belongs to—" The first time Jim spewed out this crazy notion I couldn't catch the name.

"Tanya and Boyd."

"I feel terrible. I wasn't there this week to supervise. I'm sorry. I wish—"

He actually chortled. "By all means, it's not your fault."

I breathed out. "Tanya and Boyd? No way."

"It's my worst nightmare."

My stomach tightened. "Mine too."

"Just thought you ought to know. Now it's going to hit the fan."

"Agreed." I rolled my eyes up to the ceiling.

Luke's gaze flicked to me, but he stayed quiet.

While he ordered eggs Benedict, I looked around. The restaurant was furnished like a banquet-reception room, including cream walls and buffet. Professional, crisp. The thought of food made me feel ill. I just kept wishing this huge screw-up hadn't happened.

Jim had ended the call with a timetable. The transfer of blastocyst into Belle had occurred on Friday at 3:15 in the afternoon. By nine p.m. Belle was notified of the mistake. By 9:10, Tanya was informed that her IVF transfer was aborted.

"You want to talk?" Luke produced his phone, glanced at a few messages, then set it down.

"What happens now?"

"Real world."

Luke stared at me. I stared back.

"Why am I getting the feeling you want to pull the plug?"

"Pull the plug?" His arched eyebrows suggested I was being less than helpful. He was referring to us, I know, but with the catastrophic mix-up at the lab, oddly I felt somewhat detached. He had been the one to calm me down after the phone call, and we'd fallen asleep next to each other, though my sleep was broken until I finally got out of bed around seven.

Luke slid his phone to the side as the hot plate was delivered.

"Ms. Ashton, are you sure you don't need anything?" The waitress smiled at me.

"I'm fine with—did you say Ashton? Oh no, wait a second, we're not married."

Luke's indifference stung. He could be very good at it, which probably helped in business. But it bothered me.

"Oh." The waitress sensed the rapid change between us. She

stepped forward. "That's not it. I thought you were related. Like brother and sister. Cousins—"

Luke burst into peals of laughter. "Nope. We're friends."

I couldn't stop from rolling my eyes. "Bring me pancakes," I said. "Syrup, please."

The waitress pointed to the white pitcher. "It's on the table."

"And add bacon."

Luke's face softened. "That's more like it."

Finally the waitress left us. I brushed my eyes free of stray hair. "I mean, if she had only seen us last night."

Major lean-in. Our eyes met.

"Why would she say it anyway?"

"Uh, I don't know," Luke said. "She gave me the creeps."

She covered up for assuming we were married quite nicely. I watched him cut his breakfast. I was suddenly ravenous. "As her 'professional' job, she probably works for a voodoo artist somewhere in a dark part of the French Quarter."

"That turns you off?"

"It might. If the doll had red hair."

Maple watched me cross to her reception area, her face tight with expectation.

"Thank God you're back."

I nodded and asked for Jim. He was always in first thing Monday mornings.

"Sorry, hon." She waved a hand. "Haven't seen him. About the mix-up—"

"I know, it's horrible. Wish me luck." I lifted patient files.

Her eyes grew impressively large.

"You remember they're all here for our help, right?" I gestured toward the full lobby. In every chair sat a patient or spouse, parent or friend.

Maple nodded this time. "You want me to reschedule them?"

"No, no. I'm not being sarcastic. Really. Keep with the plan for today. I just need to make one call first."

When I entered my office, my eyes dropped to the handwritten note on my desk, a list of attorneys who'd worked on fertility regulation. Understood. As the supervisor of Embryology for the merged clinics, I'd be the one who'd have to deal with any lawsuits.

I reached out to Jim by cell. Email. Text. My phone rang with a sort of recognizable number.

"Demetri?" I asked.

"Yeah. I haven't filled my days up, by any stretch. Mind if I help out?"

"Do you have ESP?" I rotated my hand, as if he could see. "Go on."

"Well, I miss work. I wish I was there."

"Couldn't have changed your mind at a better time."

"Sometimes I don't feel like I'm smart if I'm not working a thaw or grading embryos, you know? My wife wants me to grade tests."

I scribbled a note. "Why put up with that when you can be assisting with fertility?"

"Well said, boss. Be there in thirty."

I beeped Maple. "Push back the crowd, thirty minutes each, no more. Call me if Demetri's not here in precisely thirty. I'll do the first thaw now. After that, refer my patients to him for today. Send me the other staffers, except Daryl, one by one for interviews."

"I adore Demetri. And I'll do what you say, hon. Even get your lunch today 'cause you'll need it."

I suspected Maple underestimated the powerhouse combination of Emergen-C, vanilla Greek yogurt, and a Milky Way.

The call to Belle turned out differently than I expected, but it's what she'd wanted.

My legs crossed tightly, I stared at my desk. "I learned of the mix-up while I was traveling. I'm extremely sorry about this." I let my breath trail softly.

"I can't talk about this over the phone," she said.

I suggested we meet this afternoon.

"I'm teaching all day, but I could meet on Thursday."

I didn't want to wait; I was getting butterflies just thinking about going face to face. Poor thing. She'd already been through two IVF cycles and now she had to deal with this massive screw-up. "Anything you want."

"Hard Rock Café, for lunch. Please come alone, okay?"

I wasn't an actress. "Sure, anything you want, Belle. Seriously. How are you coping? If you want to abort though, I'd like to help you right away."

"No, I'm not aborting. Theo and I are meeting with a therapist."

"I was going to see if you wanted to meet with someone. It will be at our expense. You can forward the bill directly to this office."

"We can lay out the options at lunch. Thanks."

I noted the time we'd meet on Thursday. My heart was pumping as I hung up the phone. What a royal disaster. How could this have happened? If the pregnancy took, Belle would basically be like a surrogate for Tanya.

I suddenly realized that Jim didn't say what had happened to Belle's Day 5 blastocysts. I rushed to check that they were still frozen.

I phoned Dr. Sage Swan in his Manhattan office at NY Embryonic Center. While I waited for him to come on the line, I watched purplish clouds swelling, moving toward the city. Rain began falling straight, like needles.

An involuntary spasm occurred in my face, hot and direct. I felt the tremor. I felt for the cross necklace.

At this point, Dr. Swan was a man I couldn't envision. There were no pictures on the Internet. Was he short? Tall? Did he have wise creases by his eyes? A long nose? I pictured him looking like an older shepherd as I massaged my temples, waiting for his receptionist to locate him.

"Hello, Ms. Holland. How are you today?" He sounded brooding, though kind.

"Hi. I'm looking forward to meeting you soon. However, I am ready to tackle this dilemma. I'm so sorry for the patients involved and nervous for us, sir."

"Julia, your new position requires stamina." Had he been chatting with Maple? "It's going to take tenacity. Not folding when the cards aren't dealt how you want them. Even though I have been at this a long time, you are the one in charge now. Please get Chicago Live Births back on solid ground."

When I got off the phone, I did the thaw necessary for the first couple of the day, who would be going through IVF this afternoon. Maple found me and told me the blastocysts Belle harvested were indeed frozen.

I returned to my office to find Tia sitting rigidly in the armchair. Her face looked stressed and drawn, more so than when she was driving the rental in the Houston rush hour.

She didn't speak until I sat down. "I'm so nervous, Julia. This whole mess must be my fault. I'm terrified. Every time I think about apologizing to Belle and Tanya I feel sick to my stomach. I can't believe it."

"What do you mean?" I sounded like Tucker.

"You know how Fanny couldn't find Tanya's eggs?" She ran a hand through her hair. "I got confused in the reverse."

"I'm baffled," I said, studying her round face. Did Fanny play a role in the mix-up, or did she simply have the one moment of confusion? "Do you think she mixed them Day 1 when we were in Houston, or you reversed them right before the transfer?"

Her face sunk to her hands.

"Tia, talk to me."

Her chest heaved.

I circled the desk and then placed my hand on her back. "Please." I had a flash of confronting Fanny about the black market comment she made to one of the patients.

Tia raised her head. "David was off. My sister was gone, too. It was just me here. It was late. I must have grabbed T-B for Tan-ya-Boyd instead of B-T for Belle-Theodore. I must have grabbed the wrong petri. I swear I checked it but how else could this have happened? I was bombed from our trip and was trying to put in as much time as I could since we're slammed and understaffed. Susan-na's going to kill me."

A ping of guilt shot through me. We were understaffed and behind on work all the more with our travel. I cleared my throat. "I feel a loss, too. I'm speaking with Belle on Friday about her options. I hope to determine a plan forward."

"Can we change to using social security numbers like the Hous-ton clinic? I really want to keep my job."

I agreed that we needed changes and more staff. Lab security. Work ethics, especially with Fanny.

"Where was David?" I asked.

She cocked her head. "He took Susanna to the gun range that night."

The metal case. Of course. "A date?"

"I guess. Back to the mix-up, I'm really scared about the consequences and all."

"You grabbed the wrong one. We'll get through it."

It was approaching a full moon when I got home Wednesday at half past ten. There was a small package at my door. I unwrapped it.

Inside were a children's book, *Gator Gumbo*, and a card with my name on it. The first page of the book was inscribed: "For Tucker, who might be a linebacker someday. Heard all about you. Luke"

I smiled. I couldn't wait to see the little guy. The card, written in messier handwriting, read: *J, found this at the aquarium in New Orleans. Enjoy. —L.*

I read the book standing in my doorway. I liked the way the story ended: teased by a few critters, a feeble gator gets his revenge when the critters, smelling the aroma of his gumbo, fall into his pot.

I called Luke as soon as I was inside. There was a series of beeps as my call was forwarded.

"Hello?" someone asked in a husky voice. "Who's this?" His tone was almost rude.

"It's Julia Holland." I sounded like a robot.

"Oh, hey. It's Jason."

"Is Luke there?"

"No-can-do. He's in Colombia."

"Colombia—where?"

"South America."

"You're joking." Luke's words replayed in my head. "*My latest deal is, say, in a place not known for niceties.*"

Still, how'd he get there so fast? "I just got a book from him."
Hesitation.

My mind reengaged. "Ah, you sent it."

"Guilty. He bought it and asked me to mail it. He told me what
to write on the card. I swear."

While I processed this, I murmured, "Just tell Luke I called and
thank him for the book. My godson will love it."

"Fine, I'll do it."

After disconnecting I wished I'd asked other questions. When
is he back? What is he doing there? The drawing on the front of
the card was of a girl standing on her tiptoes, looking up at the two
balloons she was holding, worried one might slip from her grasp.
Jason must have bought it.

I settled into the couch, wishing Luke were beside me.

A dry wind worked me over when I stepped off the train the next
evening. The bright moonlight above was a waxing moon. The
wind also carried the smell of fine Italian food and autumn leaves. I
ambled into Beth's building.

"Tough day playing hero?" Beth said when she opened the door.

I wasn't sure if she meant IVF proceedings or mitigating the
scandal. I went with the latter, especially since I'd told her there'd
been a breach in our professionalism. "I figured out what happened.
Apparently it was accidental."

"Like somebody grabbed the wrong one?"

"Exactly. One of the employees' focus dwindled at precisely the
wrong time." It was an oversimplified explanation but a near strike.

On the kitchen counter a candle burned on either side of a water
fountain shaped like an arrangement of lilies. "Nice." I tipped my

head to the sounds. "What do you think Tucker's going to think of this?" I lifted the mesh bag containing the snorkel and mask.

"That you're reliving your childhood? The thought crossed my mind."

"Really?"

Beth turned up the heat and put a kettle on. "It's getting colder. Soon it will be the holidays." She tightened her wrap. "Any chance you'll be spending time with Luke?"

I laughed. "Are you planning to kick me out of your celebration this year?"

"Not on your life. I was wondering if I should include one extra."

The water dripping from the sculpted stamens of the fountain reminded me of the exotic flora surrounding the rooftop pool by Luke's penthouse suite. "There's this lady I know," I said, thinking of Sharon as I examined the piece, "who would love this. Do you make it on a smaller scale?"

"I could easily make it in any size you want."

The children's shouts came from somewhere in the apartment, and she glanced toward the hallway. "You're amazing," she said. "You help people conceive, and you send them a gift."

The kettle whistled, and I sighed. "Who knows?" I slid a mug across the counter to Beth. "I'll take a cup. I just wish this hadn't happened with the mix-up at work. The media are going to be all over us. I still need to meet with the patients, change our labeling policy, talk with the attorney. I wish it was as simple as helping conceive and giving a gift."

Beth shrugged.

I took the tea. "Thanks."

"Thank you for bringing the toys for Tucker." She stifled a yawn.

I visited Tucker in his room to give him the gifts I'd brought.

"That's mine?" he said.

"From my bath to yours." I bent over to hug him.

After a half hour in the big tub, with the snorkel and mask, the little guy smelled soapy, fresh, and dreamy. In his black super villain pajamas, he sat in between my legs while I played with his toes and read to him. He begged for me to read *Gator Gumbo*. His favorite part was searching each page for the gator's spoon. When he'd find it, he'd press his finger into the book so hard that the spine dug into my ankle.

"Sorry Ju-Ju," he said, squirming.

I laughed. "It's okay."

"My fault," Beth said from the doorway. "He had a cupcake at the party."

Tucker shook his head. "Na-huh. It was two." He spoke with pride.

"All right," I said, "it will be a while until you settle down. Let's go check out a website." Beth thanked me while I took Tucker down the hall into Amelie's room.

"Can we hop onto your laptop?" I asked her.

She said yes and then ignored us. I clicked open the Audubon Aquarium of the Americas in New Orleans and pulled up some marine life pictures. I found alligators. When we oohed over a screen shot of a gnarly-looking alligator, Amelie came over.

"Why's it white?" she asked.

"The caption says it's an albino."

Tucker scratched his hand through his wet hair, making it crazier still. His eyebrows arched. "What's that mean?"

I explained what "albino" meant. "They don't have camouflage like other animals, and the sun can easily burn their skin. There are less than fifty albino alligators in the world, so they're pretty rare. This one's seven years old."

"That's the ugliest thing I've ever seen." Amelie crossed her arms. She watched the photos scroll by a moment longer and then galloped back to her bed to finish a chapter book.

"I think it's cool," Tucker said. "How am I going to see it eat something?"

"Good question." I browsed through more web pages.

"If the people put a camera in its cage, we could watch it. Then I could see it eating a turtle or something else. That would be cool."

"Its eyes," I read, "are pink because its blood vessels are apparent through the see-through tissue."

"Maybe it doesn't want to live in the wild anyway."

I laughed. "I wonder if the zookeepers have thought of that. Come on, let's get you in bed or your mom's gonna fire me."

"Fire you. What's that mean?"

"Don't worry about it. I'll read you the book again."

The little guy beat me to his room. Halfway through the book, he finally yawned. After I'd finished reading, he looked up at me. "Do you think they could put a secret camera on the alligator and then YouTube it eating a turtle?"

"That sounds fun to watch?"

"Yes!"

"Maybe I'll have Luke video it when he goes back there."

"Who's Luke?"

"He gave you this book."

"Oh, right."

Twelve

THE DRUMMING OF David's fingers on Jim's desk was so rhythmic that I kept glancing out of the corner of my eye at them. Again and again I forced my attention to Jim, who was sitting across from us.

After a series of medical appointments and the advice of two specialists in the area, Jim had finally accepted his diagnosis about his recurring headaches, vertigo, and bouts with flu-like symptoms. He had Meniere's disease.

Since he worked in a clinic and was exposed to lots of different immune systems, I'd always believed it was our work environment that got to him. It was standard clinic vulnerability, but obviously not for him.

Due to the new and unfortunate diagnosis, my appointment as supervisor for Advanced Fertility National, the embryo mix-up, staffing problems, and a perceptive and protective wife, Jim would step down as supervisor of embryology at Chicago Live Births.

Jim's eyes darted toward David, who had stopped drumming. "He will take over my position."

I was livid. Before dealing with the concept of David taking over Jim's position, I gave Jim a soft look. I went around and hugged him. "I am so sorry about the Meniere's."

"Thank you, but I know I'll be leaving the clinic in capable hands. You two are the best; you're right for these jobs. These missions. I'm having a good day."

At the Hard Rock Café, Belle said nothing personal until we ordered lunch. Then she leaned forward over the table and with her hands joined she rested her chin there. "What's your take, Julia?"

"Our clinic gave you the wrong blastocysts." I indicated the points on my fingers. "We alerted you and froze your blastocysts. The couple whose embryos are implanted in you were notified. In less than two weeks we'll do the pregnancy test. That discovery will further define what we do."

I switched hands. "The positive pregnancy is easier, actually. You can carry and deliver. I'm not saying it's less invasive to you or your emotions, though. A negative pregnancy means the other couple has no chances, and the IVF failed. We could offer donor eggs to them, but let's talk about you and Theo. Immediately, we could thaw your harvested embryos, and we could implant into a surrogate female we provide because of the error. If one embryo takes inside the surrogate, you could have a baby not long after this one—Tanya's.

"If Tanya's embryo takes, then after the delivery of her fetus we could thaw and transfer your harvested embryos, implanting you . . . but it would be at least twelve months from now. However, if Tanya's embryo inside you right now doesn't take, then we'd rest your body and try implantation when you're ready. See, there's a longer and a shorter timeline. Like I said, this pregnancy test in ten days and its fate will help you and Theo rule out some of these concepts and focus on a certain path."

Belle was quiet for so long that I felt nervous I'd lost her. I hadn't.

"So I've got two main options. If I'm pregnant with Tanya's fetus, I could carry it for her and thaw my blastocysts and have a surrogate implanted with them. If I'm not pregnant with Tanya's fetus, then I should rest up and thaw, implant, and go for it on my own."

I nodded.

"How much chance do I have with thawed embryos?"

I went quiet. The Haystack salad arrived for me. Belle pulled back from the table, sat tall, and unfolded her napkin. A song by The Who played from the speakers behind me. The waitress placed a cheeseburger in front of Belle.

"Thanks," I said.

The waitress gave a thumbs-up and left.

Belle ran a hand to her lips and gathered them between her fingers.

I acknowledged her concern. "With thawed embryos, there's a slight diminishment in quality that can occur from the process. We won't know until they are looked at after the thaw."

Belle reached for the ketchup bottle, opened it, and worked some onto her plate. "I've never had a frozen cycle before." She stared out at the lunch crowd. I saw her eyes fall on a shopping bag from a store called Galt Baby. She shook her head.

"Maybe I'm not dreaming after all," she said. "I've sort of been thinking, along with Theo, that this is my shot. I've had to think about things all differently because of IVF. I always thought I'd get pregnant naturally. But no. Our family plans are prolonged even further now, but it can happen. I know it. I feel it."

She calmly lifted the burger, closed her eyes, and took a bite. She chewed, and I mixed pico de gallo into my salad. "Your patience is something I admire. I can't tell you how sorry I am for this."

"I'm sure you are, but listen, I really do want a baby who's all mine."

Our eyes met. "Listen, the potential of the embryo doesn't show until Day 5 of the embryo growth, because at that point we have a better understanding of the quality, much better than Day 3. But your Day 5 embryos were never transferred. They were both frozen. So you have those two high-quality embryos for the future and that's good."

"And if my thawed embryos are still not good enough to implant properly and result in a positive pregnancy?"

I finished a mouthful of creamy chicken, pecans, and mixed greens. "Donor eggs. That's a back-up plan if—"

"Not by a long shot. That's not a back-up for us. No donor eggs. No way. We want a baby that is all Theo and me."

With that, Belle drew her line in the sand.

I was approaching my office, looking at Maple's printout of my schedule to ensure there was a meeting with Tanya and her husband, when I glanced up and saw that the door stood ajar. There was movement inside. Thinking it was most likely my new chief embryologist, David, and not thrilled to have another distraction, I hesitated.

The sounds were definitely keyboard strokes. As I neared I could see the person's head in the reflection on the glass door. Perfect two inches of a hair bob reaching just below a pointed chin. It was Fanny.

Dubious and a little stealthy, I put my head down, tiptoed, and closed the gap in the doorway.

Fanny was sitting in a chair facing my desk now. She must have bolted across the room when she heard me. She hooked a look over her shoulder. "Hello, I was waiting for you. There's something I need to discuss with you."

"What were you doing?"

"I was curious as to why you gave Demetri his job back so fast. Don't the rest of us get some bonus for not up and quitting and then flailing and coming back? I've seen the applicant pile for this job. It's rather hefty."

"Good afternoon, Fanny." I moved into my seat, noting that the computer screen held the image it usually held: the tropical view from my parents' house. But I'd seen her sitting at my desk and heard the sounds of popping keys.

I adjusted my seat to see her better.

She shrugged. "I keep noticing that Demetri is getting all the good clients." Despite the cool direct look, a volatile bubble was building. Ping.

"You're throwing out accusations. Do you have any evidence to back this up? And what do you mean by 'good' clients?"

"Why would Demetri get all the new ones then?" Two palms shot out. "You know, ones that could be a successful first try. It's a better stat, I believe. Don't you?"

"Do you think I have a crystal ball when I choose the embryologist for a patient? And you complained recently about your workload, which I've tried to lessen."

"I'm ready for more, Julia. I'm not saying it's a dead-end job, but you and David were both promoted. I want to take on more."

That was the first I'd thought about Fanny's perspective. However, I recalled Jim's chart check and Maria Jose's stunned silence at the mention of her name.

Fanny's hands shot to her hips, slightly high because of the arms of the chair.

"Don't you think I deserve it? Now that Demetri's back and is going to get all the new patients. And he'll get a raise before me."

It was typical assertive and argumentative speak when one's agenda is thwarted.

I confronted her about the file Jim investigated; he'd only found one infraction but it was worth mentioning. "I haven't assigned you new patients because the last time you had one, the legitimacy of the embryo grades was in question."

I thought about Fanny's squeaky-clean HR file. There were no reasons listed for her being fired from the New Orleans clinic. Jim had called Maria Jose back the day I'd told him the news; it was noted that she was never reached. He didn't follow up. He could have easily forgotten Fanny's background when the New Orleans Fertility Specialists was brought up for the merger.

"Anyway, I'd prefer if you didn't infer about Demetri or any of the others for that matter," I said.

Fanny wagged a finger back and forth. "You'll see. I'm the best one you've got. I stand behind my grading."

This was going nowhere.

She kept going. "By the time you find some good staff to work for us, there'll be more than a mix-up to deal with. Tia's stressed and Susanna's close behind. Daryl should be working at a Starbucks."

"Hey, that's enough, Fanny."

I recalled Daryl's question about Fanny: "How did she get a job at CLB?"

She thought a moment. "Do you know your computer was making some strange noise when I came in, and I corrected it for you? Who do you think fixed the speakers in the lab? David Lazel and his smarmy attitude?"

I sliced a hand through the air. "Enough."

Three days later, on the afternoon of November twelfth, I remembered it was closing night for *A Midsummer Night's Dream* at the Shakespeare Theatre. I had to hurry to make the play.

Slipping into my seat, I received a few glares for my late entrance.

On the stage, the moon—a disco ball flashing purple neon—descended through the woods. The moonlight finally settled into gold. It made me think of the real full moon and how it was affecting my sleep. I kept catching myself closing my eyes during the first act.

During intermission I mingled and listened to the crowd's confusion over what was really happening with the fairies and all the lovers. And the donkey head that replaced the head of Bottom, which then scared the workmen senseless. However, he began to sing such a sensuous song that the queen of the fairies woke up and fell hard for him.

In a later act, in another forest scene, Puck asked the audience if they were watching a play that was being performed or if it was all a dream.

I stared down at Janie dressed as Hippolyta and Harrison dressed as Greek royalty. All of the players were somehow connected and drawn to these two for the chance to celebrate at their wedding. I could see Janie's rosy glow—what a gorgeous girl.

Later in her dressing room, I hugged Janie. "You were incredible. Harrison too; he's as unbelievable as you are."

"No Pier."

I knew Pier was the name they'd wanted for the baby and probably they discussed it when they were out on a date at Navy Pier. "What happened?" I swallowed. "Did the pregnancy end?"

Her eyes were so sad and heavy. I wrapped my arms around her. She sobbed.

"Harrison dumped me."

"What?"

I held her a long moment. When she tried to talk, her voice came out as a scratchy whisper. "I should just get an abortion, shouldn't I?"

"That's the last thing you should do. Wow, I thought you guys were in love. It's so abrupt." I lifted her chin. "You can do this, Janie. I believe you can. Promise me you'll sleep on it for at least a week." I handed her another tissue. And waited. "You need some rest, my friend."

Thirteen

THE FOLLOWING WEEK the moon waned to a fledgling and resembled a sunken boat floating in darkness. As usual, I slept more peacefully with the shift.

Thursday morning dawned windy and gray-skied. Outside the Soho breakfast room, the Manhattan throng moved briskly. Hair swirled around narrowed eyes in the wind gusts.

Sage Swan texted at eight. The meeting was set for ten, but he wanted to know if I could meet earlier. Issues with merger updates required his presence around noon. I let him know that I would be happy to meet him at the clinic as soon as I could get there.

By half past eight, I'd grabbed a toasted English muffin and jam and was in a cab scooting toward Park Avenue. The air was thick with the smell of blackberry preserves and musty seats.

When the cab driver dropped me off, I checked out the Midtown building that housed the laboratory and clinic. The modern front looked inviting. I'd already located Sage's office from the Internet listing, but I went up to the receptionist and introduced myself.

Since I was anticipated—not just for today, but as a leader in the laboratory for the overall conglomerate—the administrator jumped up from her seat. "Hi, I'm Marybeth."

Though the waiting area was packed with patients, she grabbed another receptionist from an alcove decked with printers, copiers, and filing cabinets to cover her position.

Marybeth escorted me outside the welcome area to an elevator, then onto the uppermost floor. Finally, she led me across a long hall to Sage Swan's spacious, well-lit medical suite. He had great views of Madison Avenue and the city beyond. A large bottle of water and two impressive computer monitors sat on his vast desk. Marybeth kept chattering. Without being obvious, I studied the man behind the glass wall as he talked with an older woman, who was probably my parents' age.

Swan's demeanor was direct and favorable. He didn't rush her though I knew he could sense that we were in the vicinity. Her image from the back reminded me of Beth in a few ways: the lanky upper body and the tailored vintage clothes, her slender neck and short, dark layered hair. Her long legs were crossed at the ankles, and she wore patent low wedges, despite the chilly weather.

After nodding absently to something Marybeth said, I silently recounted my view of the wise shepherd and amended it to a retired CEO of a Fortune 500 company. Swan's glasses were sleek and contemporary. His salt-and-pepper hair was neatly trimmed, and his eyes seemed to lead his entire body as if a hunger was behind them.

After formally bidding good day to the visitor, Swan walked her out the door himself. Then he got straight to us. "Well, hello. You are not at all how I envisioned you."

A flush erupted across my face.

"I think you are even more studious and bodacious than that, but after all, is bodacious really a word?"

"Please take a seat. Make yourself comfortable. Thanks, Marybeth." He waved her goodbye.

I liked his enthusiasm. "I believe bodacious is a combination of bold and audacious," I said, "and I don't hear it that often anymore."

"I'll keep that in mind. My grandchildren say 'awesome' with a feverish regularity. I'm afraid it'll slip when I'm with my associates." Even though Swan could retire anytime, it might well be that the younger embryologists relied on him regularly for guidance and perhaps confidence too.

"Well as long as you don't say 'radical,' or worse 'rad,' you're okay with me."

His eyes tightened. "That's not even in my vocabulary." He chuckled. "But watch me start using it. My rad associates and I welcome you." His arms unfolded and reached out. "It's good to finally meet you in person, Julia. How are you dealing with the snafu in Chicago?"

"With kid gloves."

He gestured for me to continue.

"I'm frustrated. Until the pregnancy test, I can't do anything, you know? Because Tanya met with Jim right away, I know she is emotional too. Her body won't have the pitfalls of the pregnancy symptoms but she addressed her biggest concern, not having the bonding. She feels robbed of that, not able to talk to the fetus, feel the movements and rhythms either. I don't know."

After a pause, we moved onto the actions we'd taken. "We busted our tails to get the labeling changed to the new format, without any major modifications in the patients' IVF schedules. That wasn't easy."

"Tell me about the other transition. Jim's new appointee."

I reminded myself that I couldn't let my frustrations get in the way. "I always stand behind Jim's decisions. Even if it doesn't make total sense to me; he appointed David Lazel as supervisor at CLB."

"Why do you say that?"

"You know Jim. He's a fabulous mentor and the most trustworthy person out there. Maybe David is the best choice among our staff in Chicago. He's strong-willed and very smart."

"And?"

"I can't tell whether he's more cocky or opportunistic. He was there at the merger announcement. He's always in the right place at the right time."

Swan gave a quick smile. "Until the night of the mix-up. I know you were in New Orleans. Where was David?"

"From what I was told, he was done working for the night. He took another staffer to the gun range."

That night in the bath I twisted my toes around the faucet, tagging off each drip with my big toe. I couldn't stop wondering why I was so irritated about David's appointment. Not being a part of the decision-making process, I guessed.

Keep your friends close and enemies closer. Was Fanny my friend or my foe? She had come down with a cold, but it seemed she could have made it to the New York clinic. She wanted a promotion, but she only did the minimal to get by. Maybe she really was feeling too bad. She'd been so excited about the trip.

The water temperature reminded me of Luke's heat-packed towels that night in New Orleans. I missed him. I twisted my hair into a knot and grabbed a clip and secured it, and then sank lower into the suds and hot water.

Liquid love. *What was Fanny's reference about?* Mysterious David. It was Tia who said something about Fanny not being "all that much trouble," that I needed to worry more about David. But Susanna had gone shooting with him at the gun range.

I struggled to find a balance. Jim was passing on the torch to those he mentored. Nothing wrong with that. David had been opportunistic—helping Jim with his doctor's appointments and supporting him, all the while pitching his intelligence. He was smart. Clever. I had to admire him. I just always thought I would be the one to take over for Jim, and felt some envy over that. I had to let it go because it was foolish. I was in charge of it all.

Tucker's question popped into my head: Do you think they could put a secret camera on the alligator and then YouTube it eating a turtle? I closed my eyes and thought of the little guy. Despite the floral scent of the bubble bath I imagined the fishy odor of a gator.

Surveillance.

Secret camera.

Catching gator-eating rodents.

I recalled the image online of the gator's ancient-looking jaws snapping closed. I heard the bubbles sifting around as I raised my arms through the water, breaking the surface. I opened my eyes.

I took a towel from the rack and dried the water from my face. It still bothered me that I wouldn't really ever know whether Fanny switched the embryos on Day 1 or Tia mistakenly did it on Day 5. I'd know if I'd had a camera in my lab.

As I was drying off, Sam called.

"Hi Racy, how you're doing?"

"Don't call me that. I'm thinking—slowly—because the hot bath just went to my head."

"Where are you?"

"Manhattan."

"Ha! There's like a million things to do there, and taking a bath is the least obvious. What's going on?"

"Well, Luke's in Colombia."

"Reality check. Huh? You're in New York, and he's away on business."

"That's right. What's on your mind really?"

"I thought of something while I was working. Didn't you say that Luke's bodyguard has a background in security? Of pearls?"

"Yeah." I said. My gator surveillance thought returned. I dried down to my feet, trying not to drop the phone.

"Jason does security. Call him and maybe he could help you figure out a way to install a hidden camera. Then you can keep your eye on the people there. And of course the embryos!"

Fourteen

A CAREFULLY MEASURED glass of red wine helped me decompress a little, but it wouldn't prevent me from speaking to Jason with clarity about the lab security issue.

Hearing a friendly-sounding hello, I announced myself. I perched on the edge of the couch, feeling self-conscious all of a sudden.

"Are you in New York?"

"I'm here, but he's not back."

"When does he return?" I asked.

"Later this week."

I frowned. I'd be back in Chicago again. "Why aren't you with him?"

"He has other protection. I have to leave it at that." He paused. "Let's just say that—"

We both laughed; it was how Luke talked.

"Well . . . well—" I couldn't remember how I was supposed to start.

"What do you want to ask? Something about Luke, I presume."

"No, it's about my godson, who is infatuated with gators. He wants to set a secret camera to tape them eating big rodents. It sounds crazy, but it got me thinking about the security at my labs. That maybe I should install security cameras. What do you think?"

"How old is your godson?"

I scrunched my forehead. "Four."

"Okay, matches up. I've got a nephew about that same age. His name is Heath."

"I bet he's afraid of you."

"Why do you say that?"

"Because you're in the security business and you might be way too perceptive. I bet Heath can't get away with anything."

"You kind of got me pegged. But Heath is fearless and maybe a little too clever. We'll see. I love the kid."

There was a moment of awkward silence.

"Let's meet," Jason said. "I can explain a couple of different options for lab protection."

"I have to work with the research team at the clinic here for the next two days." I had to finish up a really important analysis of unexplained infertility in couples under thirty-five. "There's no wiggle room in my schedule."

"How about right now?"

It was 9:20. I stood up. "Okay, name a place. Something that's easy to find."

He told me he would text me.

My hair was a tangle from the humid bath. I quickly braided and tied the end. Then I threw on a violet blouse with dark jeans, boots, and a jacket.

Famous for its baked goods and seafood bar, the restaurant Baltha-zar sits on the corner of Crosby Street and Spring. It reminded me of the sophisticated French restaurant I loved so much in Chicago.

I found Jason behind a pillar, near the zinc bar.

"You want security?" he asked.

"Hello to you, too." I sat across from him. "That's why I came."

I settled my purse and jacket, and then spotted his dark cocktail. Obviously, he was off duty.

"I'm quite versed on safety and protection. I can talk about some things. Back in the Philippines the farmers of the Golden South Sea Pearls do nothing to fortify the nacre or culture the pearls faster that I'm aware of. So, you can imagine their growth is a precious thing to preserve. And any number of threats can crop up."

"I've come to the right guy then." I smiled and crossed my legs. "I guess Luke's place in the city is more than meets the eye?" I winked. "Hidden cameras everywhere?"

"If you make that assumption."

"One might just do that. I'm a little nervous about the labs. Another instance of tampering or even an accident—if it's as big a deal as the mix-up—could destroy the whole clinic."

His dark eyes twinkled. "Get clearance, approval, whatever you need for a work order, and I can be in Chicago. Just say the word."

We each ordered chocolate desserts, copying the people at the table next to us. We'd smelled the rich cocoa wafting our way. I also ordered an Irish cream.

He sat back, eyes dulling a little. The shift was slight.

"Now," he passed the menus back to our waiter and chuckled at me. "It's my turn to go fishing. Luke wants you in the city as his date for a wedding . . . his friends Charlie and Darla."

This was starting to be weird, but I asked the date of the wedding anyway.

"Sure."

"Great, I'll let him know."

"Oh, not actually yes, I need to see if that would coincide with a trip to our New York clinic. I've got a lot going on, and any time away has to be for a real good reason."

"Don't worry." His sparkling eyes returned. "I won't tell Luke you put it that way."

"He would understand, yes?"

"Of course. You're so serious, Julia."

Our desserts came, and we both took a couple forkfuls.

What was he referring to? I frowned. "Well in any case, serious or not, let me ask you another thing in confidence. Do you know a guy by the name of David Lazel or how Luke might know him?"

"I can't discuss Blackwater in specifics." He'd said it once before, but he apparently wanted me to understand that he really couldn't.

Jason was leaning sideways over the table and took his cell phone from his pocket.

"I hear you." The law of diminishing returns set in, something my professor father had warned of when it came to eating sweets, and no more chocolate soufflé would increase my satisfaction. I pushed the plate aside. "That was very good."

"Mine too. What else can I help you with?" he said lazily.

"I don't intend to keep you up all night with my questions, though I feel they are important." I was sharp. More than I intended.

He laughed, shaking his head. "You give redheads a whole new buzz."

"Thanks."

"You mentioned David Lazel, but that doesn't ring a bell. Who is he?"

"Guy from work. He acts buddy-buddy with me. He says he'll do anything to help out with recoding to socials."

Jason looked puzzled.

"He helped Demetri, Daryl, Jim, and me with a very serious project in the lab. We were quiet to concentrate. No Sinatra from the speakers this time. No one dared talk or distract anyone else. Except David. You know what? He was buttering me up, and Jim too."

"Brownie point sandwich."

"What's that mean?"

"He's kissing up. Maybe trying to take over." He laughed.

"The embryo world," I muttered. I crossed my arms and leaned on the table. "David mentioned knowing Luke from Blackwater. He tried to shock me with his name, but then he clammed up and refused to say anything else. Maybe he can't for some reason. But it made me even more curious about Luke's past."

Jason palmed his left cheek. I thought he might be pondering what he could and couldn't say.

All this time I'd been so focused on Luke, I hadn't really paid attention to this man's appearance. But his brooding, military style, the unperfected scar on his right cheek. I had trouble not staring into his intense, coal-black eyes.

He stood up. "Excuse me, I'll be right back." He looped around a few tables to go to the men's room.

Golden South Sea Pearls were very pretty; I'd viewed some online at jewelry sites. Colombia didn't have pearls. What could Luke be doing there?

I stared at Jason's phone, wondering what knowledge he'd password protected.

He returned quickly. "You mentioned speakers for music. In the lab, right?"

I nodded.

"That's as good a place as any for surveillance. They're already mounted."

"Nope, try again. They're fickle, and both David and a technician are messing with them."

I asked more about Luke.

He finally let his guard down. "Blackwater was his employer. But he's not a mercenary or a private contractor. He was employed there to work on numbers and ideas. He saved them some major dough. Although he was promoted rapidly, he wanted his own company to drive profit, have some skin in the game.

"And honestly, I've never heard of David Lazel, but I have to admit I've heard Luke mention Will Lazel, who he worked with in North Carolina at Blackwater. He said he was always at the training facility. Maybe he was an instructor or something. But Luke worked at a high-rise in Virginia back then."

"Hmm, thanks. I didn't know any of that." I told him I would be in touch about the labs and with an answer for the wedding weekend.

"We'll see you in Chicago."

Later, when I was settled into my room, I slipped into my old pajamas again and crawled into bed. I pulled a down comforter to my ears and slept.

Fifteen

REILLY'S BAR CLOSED for a renovation, so Luke and Jason showed up at my place. It was three days after my New York trip and the day before Belle would do her blood draw for the pregnancy results for Tanya and Boyd. Outside my living room window the dusk was just beginning to push through a band of tangerine and pink.

Luke hugged me passionately. Jason gave a quick wave hello. We sat around the large coffee table with its bowls of shells and sand-colored starfish. Jason rocked a fast pace in my only rocking chair.

"Heard it's supposed to snow tomorrow." Luke slipped his loafers off.

"Me, too."

Jason took out his phone and glanced at the screen. He and Luke shared a look. I used the moment to catch Luke off guard. "Why is he," I thumbed toward Jason, "asking me out for you? You can call from Colombia. It's a free country."

He laughed a contrary *ha*! "It was just precautionary."

My scowl kept growing.

"Danger, my dear."

He looked devious and totally hot, and I didn't trust him at all. I tossed my hair back, trying to think clearly.

He bent closer. Sweet hops on his breath sailed my way as he brought his face to mine and kissed me. When I opened my eyes, Jason had vanished.

When Jason left to do research on camera installation in the lab, Luke and I were alone. Immediately he had to take a call, and I made the mistake of going over my "calendar at a glance."

"I'd like to know more about you," I said when Luke returned to the living room. "Jason shared some things."

"I trust he did."

"Where'd you find that?"

He was holding red wine in the hand-blown glass from my mother's sea glass shop. She sent me one or two for Christmas every year.

"Wine or the glass?" He laughed. He held the turquoise-, olive-, and hummus-colored glass, the stem and stand aquamarine. "This is particularly nice. I've never encountered one like it before."

"My mom has been hunting down sea glass since she was a child. She keeps everything she finds. When my dad used to work a lot on his research at night she took classes in glassblowing. She has her own shop."

"Hmm, she sounds like you."

"She is." I thought about my mother, who was gorgeous, the part not at all like me. "Mostly like me. I could tell you all about her, or you could meet her sometime. They're in Florida."

"What part?"

"The Keys." I took the glass he offered and drank with a flourish. I stared at him. "I know a sandy spot I could take you to."

"I like your type. You don't notice anything but your work, until—"

He swept me up.

Every one of my synapses was on edge as he carried me down the hall. I guessed it was just his pull on me. When we got to my bedroom, he placed me gently on my bed. I closed my eyes as he sucked the fingers on my right hand. Then he moved to my left hand. I moaned. I felt hot.

"You're my man." My eyes shot open in panic. "I meant *kind* of man. You're my *kind* of man!"

He smiled at me, sort of a game-winning look.

"Stop that. You didn't win."

"I did, because you can't change what you said."

He

You start with a butterfly needle and the freshest-looking vein. I'd watched nurses do this a thousand times. Belle had probably had it done by nurses two dozen times. She sat tall and very still in front of the nurse and the rest of us; it was the moment we had all been waiting for. Worry was easy to see in the crinkles between her eyes. One fist was curled in a ball. Theo stood with her, holding the free hand.

I'd met with Tanya earlier, and she was getting more adjusted. We were paying to have her see a therapist to deal with her emotional feelings. She thanked me for that.

Belle's nervous behavior was exactly what I'd anticipated. She'd told me on the way to the room where we were drawing her blood that she wanted to move on the idea of a surrogate for her own blastocysts.

David entered the drawing room and introduced himself to the patients. "Are you ready for this?"

Belle nodded.

"See you this afternoon for follow-up," he said to me. "I'd like to help you, if you need it. I can return any calls to the press or talk to the supervisors at the other clinics."

"Sure, that would work." He commanded the room, gazing at me intently. I felt that he understood the dire position we were in as a clinic.

When David left, I watched the needle dart below the skin by the smooth handiwork of the nurse, Gertie. Belle took short breaths and squeezed the ball of her hand tighter. The vial filled with crimson blood.

After Gertie withdrew, I took control. "Are you implying you want to get a surrogate regardless of the outcome?"

"I'm not implying; I'm for sure."

"Why not?" I smiled. "We are in favor of however you want it to go."

Gertie left to test the blood.

"There are a number of reasons, but the most important one is that I can feel I am pregnant, and I'm sure this blood test will tell you so. I am happy to carry it for this other patient, but I want the same for me. For a while I wasn't sure, but now I am. I believe the mix-up was an accident, and I can help out. And someone can help me. It's fair."

Theo's eyes swept the room, stopping at me. "I agree with everything she's saying," he said. "It's not tit for tat, but it's something like that."

I laughed at his unplanned rhyme. "Loose ends," I said. "We really are so very sorry."

The blood would have to be put on a machine to get an actual number. I left for a half hour and then returned to wait with Belle and Theo. A few minutes after I joined them, a couple of raps came at the door. My arm hairs prickled. Gertie poked her head in. She held up a thumb. "Numbers are strong." She looked at me, tipped her head. "Very high."

"Are you saying it's a fetus?"

I took Belle's hands. "Yes, yes. Thank you for doing an enormous favor. Thank you." I held my breath should she change her mind. "It's twins. That's what Gertie means. Two fetuses in you."

Belle withdrew from me, placing a hand over her arm where the blood was drawn, blocking her abdomen. "How? Are you sure?"

I had to let out my breath.

"Not yet," said Gertie. "But numbers that high are usually telltale."

"Theo, what do you think?" asked Belle.

"Why are you asking me?"

I watched Belle narrow her eyes. She directed her focus toward me. "In retrospect, I realize I said I would carry if it was positive, but this is not what I bargained for."

I offered her a hand. She turned and grabbed Theo. He hauled her from the seat and whisked her from the room.

Sixteen

"WHAT ARE YOU suggesting," I said, "a way to beat the Face-Time application?" I always thought it wasn't the best way to see the caller.

Luke didn't dispute my question. "I wanted to tell you that you inspire me," he said, "and being with you in the French Quarter gave me the best idea. I call it the Sleeping Idea. I watched you sleeping, and . . ." he lowered his voice to nearly a whisper.

I strained to hear him, as I was on the busy sidewalk outside Beth's townhome in Chicago. He alluded to some secret invention that everyone would want someday. Like the smartphone.

"I'll call you again soon, I promise. Bye, sweets." Then he was gone.

When I reached Beth's penthouse, I knocked a few times. No one answered, so I dug around in my purse. I found the notes I'd made on the train a long while ago about Hiatus and my idea to house IVF patients on a resort island. And then I found the key she'd given me. I let myself in and waited. It wasn't long before I found myself at their kitchen counter, perched on one of the pewter barstools, flipping through Hiatus notes. In an email, I made a bulleted list and then shot it to Sage Swan. And for good measure, I copied Maria Jose, another person I respected in the new conglomerate.

I heard the front door open and close. Beth entered the kitchen. "Sorry that took forever. The clients were undecided, split between a large waterfall and a more average size, but ultimately the space will dictate, once they get around to measuring. How are you?"

"I'm okay. Luke rang me from Colombia, a whopping two-minute call."

"What did he say?"

"Not much, just inspired on his end, I guess."

I grabbed the top puzzle from the game shelf in the kitchen. "I'll get going on this. Where are Amelie and the little guy?"

"Tommy got off work early. Can you believe it? He surprised the kids and took them for pizza."

"Sounds fun." I tried not to sound disappointed. "I wish there was another Dave Matthews show."

She laughed. "You too?"

I dumped out the puzzle and started flipping pieces over. It was a brightly colored world map, with countries and tiny symbols of their exports. I knew Tucker liked it, whereas Amelie rarely joined until the border was complete. She was then some kind of puzzle piece genius. If they were out late with Tommy, they'd probably have to go to bed shortly after they were back, but I could leave the puzzle half finished.

"Luke is a stand-up guy," Beth said as she handed me a glass of wine.

"And he still seems to be interested in me." I took a sip. "Which is a modern miracle."

"Give yourself some credit. You're a knockout! I've been saying it forever."

I laughed. "Right." I joined a whale head and tail along the northern border. Antarctica was coming together.

I started to tell Beth about what I'd said to Luke at my place, staking a claim on him right in the vulnerable moment, but I picked up a piece belonging in South America. "This mean anything to you?" I rotated the puzzle piece.

"What is it?"

"It's from Colombia. Says part of the name here. See?" The squared off puzzle piece showed a green rectangular stone as one of five symbols for the country. The others included textiles, coffee, oil, and flowers.

"Emeralds." Her almond-shaped eyes held mine a moment. Carpe Diem.

That was it. "That's what Luke is there for." Precious gems, mine them, set a value. Positioning for a new ETF.

I pulled my iPad from my bag. Beth hung over my shoulder. I should have seen that, but I'd just been so preoccupied.

The first page that came up described how an increase in global demand for the green stones allowed for prices to almost double in the early twentieth century. The rest of the content wasn't glitzy: Strife. Jungle wars. Long-term unrest.

I read aloud: "Today, the Colombian emerald trade is engrained at the center of Colombia's civil conflict that has plagued the country since the 1950s."

"Luke's into all that?" Beth gulped. "You better pray he has protection."

"He has a bodyguard—who didn't go to Colombia with him, so I don't know what to tell you."

A loud trio came bellowing through the front door. A full minute passed before their shoes were piled and bags dropped, then they entered the kitchen. I looked up from the screen.

I smelled the pepperoni. I saw smiles and Amelie holding Tucker's hand. Tommy pretended to walk a tight rope, balancing two brown cardboard boxes on his head. He got close and stopped. The boxes slid down onto Beth's palms. "Thank you. We're starving." She winked at me. "You all are just in time to help Julia with the world puzzle."

"I don't like going at it solo."

A stool screeched over, and Tucker climbed in beside me, close. "Thanks, buddy." I rubbed his soft hair. "How was dinner?"

"My belly hurts. I had too much root beer."

Beth returned with plates and frowned at Tommy. He shrugged.

I didn't realize I was still holding the Colombia piece.

"I'll take that." Amelie grabbed the piece from my hand and examined it. "That's my birthstone."

Tucker said, "What's that mean?"

"My birthday's in May." Amelie tilted her head and smiled proudly.

Later, I tried to rub Tucker's back until he fell asleep. My mind was racing as I told him about places in the world I'd visited. "I went scuba diving in Belize and Australia. I like coral reefs."

"Have you been to where the birthstone for Amelie is?"

I shook my head and then realized he couldn't see. "No, baby. It's in South America. And you know my boyfriend, Luke, who I told you about? Well, he's there, back and forth on business." From what I'd read with Beth about the negative byproducts of the Colombian emerald trade, Luke was right to exercise caution. Colombia was not a free country, not at all. He didn't want his phone to be traced back to me. I felt a thrill. He wanted to protect me.

I rubbed the fuzz on Tucker's upper neck where the hairline met his scalp. He looked up at me. I only saw the sparkling lights of his eyes. Love—it's a . . . tricky thing. I kissed the little guy's cheek.

"Take me on an adventure, please."

"I will someday, I promise." For some reason New York popped into my head, and I found myself telling him about the Statue of Liberty, the art museums, and the American Museum of Natural History. "We could even grab a friend named Heath who's also your age. That's my friend Jason's nephew. It would be fun."

His eyes were big and I knew I wasn't helping to lower his excitement level. "Hey, I'll rub your back."

Later, when I tiptoed out, all of the Ramsays were snug, and the house was wrapped in peaceful quiet.

Back home, I plugged in my phone after seeing that there weren't any messages. I nearly made it until three a.m., when I turned over and felt chilled. I pulled up a blanket and was still lying there an hour later, picturing Theo and his huge upper body, holding a golf bag and his hand on his hip, squinting to see where his ball landed. Would he find it? I swallowed and wondered how they were doing tonight. Was Belle comfortable or did she have nausea? Could she keep the emotions of twins from chipping away at her rational thoughts? Knowing they belonged to Tanya and Boyd?

I felt bleak.

I switched to thinking about Luke, but that turned into a Colombian jungle vision. But I recalled what the Internet search revealed about the emeralds, those stones that were the most sought after and desirable. Shimmery and beautiful. Brilliant green. Only found in the deepest mines in the mountains of Colombia. Muzo mine. It was one of the three most prized sources—and could likely be the most dangerous as well. Its location was in the eastern portion of the Andes Mountains, notable for its particularly rare sedimentary rock embedded in the emerald deposits.

Not too much later, I exploded from a dream. I pushed back the covers. My neck and forehead were wet. In the dream I had been in my lab, working on grading embryos, and Tanya had dashed in and shouted, "Twins don't work for me."

⟨◎⟩

No Sinatra music bled from the lab speakers the following evening.

I sorted sounds. Fanny was telling David she'd finish up. Susanna was tapping on a keyboard, entering data on embryo grades. A door opened as David left. Then Fanny's voice again: "Dream Fertility called. I'll plug them in for next Wednesday."

Before I could object, she was out of the room.

Susanna took three steps, then paused.

She said she'd clean the workstations. A backward elbow jab, then she smiled. "I'm happy to check the incubator too."

Striding with purpose, she began the rounds.

After expressing appreciation, I went out to the hallway and grabbed the elevator to my office. Once there my phone broke the stillness.

"Miss Holland. Is that you?"

"Yes, who is this?"

No response.

"Who is this?"

The voice came again, louder. "Miss Holland? We'd like to talk to you."

"Okay, what's this about?" A person from the news? A staff embryologist at another lab?

Nothing.

"I'm still here."

No one spoke up.

I stepped to my desk and then around. I drew the blinds, feeling self-conscious. I watched the blinds fall. Then I heard a deep breath.

Why was I holding?

A text beeped in. Sam.

The heat kicked on, but I began to shiver anyway.

I was about to disconnect when I heard pleading, "You've got to help us, Miss Holland. It's Violet. We really are desperate for a baby. Both of us. We'll do anything."

I put the name with a face. Violet was the potential patient who carried around the book *What to Expect When You're Expecting*.

Seventeen

"YOU ARE THE expert. You have the highest success rates. We've checked. This is Violet Champion and my husband Dylan."

Dylan cleared his throat and said, "Hello." His voice was deep.

"Violet, we talked about getting your information from Dream Fertility. Maple from our office made three attempts, but we were never sent your records."

"Dylan and I were still pretty upset about the treatment at Dream Fertility, and we've been working through it."

Out of the corner of my eye, I saw an email pop to the center of my laptop screen. Terror froze me in that spot.

The subject line read: "Are you playing GOD?"

"Violet, Dylan, we can help, so please do yourself a favor and inquire with Maple. She would be happy to schedule you. I should be in town Monday through Thursday next week. Now I must go."

I maximized the inbox.

It started off, "We mean you harm because of all the harm and manipulation you do to human life." The other terrifying part said, "The only way to change your ego and your path of destruction is for us to get back at you. We may steal embryos and donor eggs from your main clinic. You can't possibly fix all the infertile people. Because if you could, you would be GOD."

I stared at the bottom.

"The Embryo Clinic" was the strangest calling card ever.

I called David Lazel.

"I'm finishing up at the gun range," he said. "If I don't stay in the rotation, all the other dudes are gonna jump in front of me."

"Fine, practice shooting. We've just gotten a serious threat. We may need your skills soon."

"Say what?"

I brought up a Google search while he waited out a series of gunshots.

"I'm searching for other 'The Embryo Clinic' threats. Have you ever heard of it?"

"Julia, what, are you crazy?"

"I'm calling Sage if you can't call your practice off!" Finally, I heard him tell someone to go ahead of him. Again he asked if I was crazy, his voice barely audible over the gun cracking.

Distressed, I sorted options. I saw no results in my search. Could the email be traceable? The address looked like gibberish. My "mix-up" patients were barely willing to go the distance with delivery of twins. Luke was not going to be able to help me. Nor could anyone for that matter.

And merely minutes ago there were Violet and Dylan: "We really are desperate for a baby." She implored me to aid her. Would Violet steal donor eggs? I practically sent the thought shooting out my office door. All of this *was* making me cuckoo.

I heard David scuffling around. Clicking a case open and then shut.

"I'm on my way. I'm nearly out the door."

I nodded. "I'll be here."

Thirty seconds later I was in the embryology lab. Susanna had left the incubator and workspace in great shape. I dropped onto a stool and waited for David.

"Why are you always at the gun range?"

"Clearly your adrenaline is still pumping. I don't suppose my father getting gunned down by an armed robber when I was a kid would be a good enough answer for you."

"Oh, I'm sorry."

I spent the next few minutes concentrating on understanding David. And getting a grip on my nerves.

He seemed to appreciate my attention.

Darkness had settled by the time I felt calm enough to gather my thoughts on our precautionary steps. Clarity, almost. Being nearly threatened once and for sure threatened after that will force it, I guess.

Nevertheless, we got to work.

We debated the significance of "main" in reference to which of our five clinics was being targeted. David thought "The Embryo Clinic" threat was probably referring to the Chicago lab since the letter came to me. I didn't agree. The New York Embryonic Center came to my mind. The largest egg donor supply was there. Or the use of "main" was a ploy and one of the smaller donor departments would be the real target.

We were still perplexed by the part saying we couldn't "fix all the infertile people." We'd never claimed that we could. What clinic would? The merger situated us as a powerhouse but not a money-back-guarantee baby-producer. And where was the logic in stealing donor eggs?

"We are vulnerable," David said. "You're right."

"Well, for one thing, we never received a threat like this before the merger."

I reflected on Jim's effective leadership. "To our knowledge."

"Good point. I'll talk to Jim. Maybe there have been threats and we just don't know."

Still, I was bothered by the singling out of my inbox.

David did the rub-and-scratch move over his beard.

I uncrossed my legs and leaned toward him.

"I remember a conversation I had with Susanna about Tia."

I wanted to smack him. I walked to the window and placed my hands on the windowsill and took several breaths. He was egotistical, callous, and clearly dating our employee, which was against company rules, but I had yet to unearth an immoral fiber in his character. By his stardom recently and flawless championing of Jim's position, he was a definite asset in our future.

End of story: I would have to trust him.

I turned and faced him. "I can get us better security in all of our labs."

He raised his eyebrows.

"Through Luke and his guy." If I was dating Luke and Luke had a bodyguard, then couldn't I convince both Luke and the bodyguard that they needed to help me secure the labs? Would it be taking advantage?

David shot me a look of appreciation. "Fine, and I'll try not to . . . hit on you."

Susanna must be wrapped around his finger. "Puh-leeze keep your girlfriend completely silent about the surveillance, and tell her nothing more. It would be counterproductive."

He raised his palms. "But you can talk to your boyfriend," he pretended to whine.

Before I could say anything David looked at his watch. "Let's get out of here. Totally separate." He winked at me.

Eighteen

THERE WASN'T AN empty seat in the waiting room. Sipping my vanilla latte, I checked the schedule board by Maple's phone, then picked up a dry-erase marker and made a note by Violet's name. She'd called fifteen minutes after we opened. And again. And a third time.

I then listened to my voicemails. There was one from Meaghan Wilson, who sounded thrilled. She said it was urgent that I see her first thing today. I took down her number.

There was a message from embryologist Sara Lance from Dream Fertility. She sounded formidable and frustrated at the same time. She knew I was in town this week and hoped to meet up this Wednesday.

And there was a message from my mother, who also sounded formidable and frustrated. She said, "Call me back. Your father wants to put the house up for sale."

Maple saw me scribbling and said, "Sharon and Trey sent flowers. I set the vase on your desk. They loved the water sculpture you sent for the baby shower."

"That's so sweet of them." I paused, felt my eyebrows knitting. "Who is Meaghan Wilson?"

Maple smiled grandly. "She's right behind you. She's Belle's surrogate."

"Hello." I stretched out my hand. Meaghan shook firmly.

Once I'd led her to one of the green patient rooms, just past the waterfall sculpture and atrium, we settled in. Meaghan had opted for an inflatable workout ball as her seat. Maple's grand smile had nothing on Meaghan. She was like a monkey in a zoo when the zoo-keeper came for feeding time, all tricks and rewards.

"This is great," she waved a hand. "And I like the natural colors in here. Very feng shui."

"Thank you. Welcome. I am pleased to meet you."

On the workout ball, she rolled out and in about six inches, out and in, as we chatted. Her abdomen unflinching. "Thank you, I'm enthusiastic about being here."

"I'm sure you've been alerted to the situation."

She nodded. "I'm told Belle is carrying a set of twins for another patient." Her eyes were wide, telling me she admired Belle.

"She's a charitable person. We're thankful."

Waving a hand again, Meaghan told me she knew she would be stimulated for the implantation of Belle's blastocysts.

After we covered the timeline of birth control to get her cycle set up and prepped her on the estrogen and progesterone meds, I told her it would be about two weeks to implantation and then asked if she had any concerns.

"Nope. Just a question about Belle and Theodore. What's their last name?"

"Harting."

"That's good, we're not related. I have cousins with the last name Harding. I just wanted to ensure I wouldn't have any issues there. I look forward to meeting them."

Her core worked with the ball's movements. I'd probably fall right off it with that kind of motion. She seemed down-to-earth and professional. "How many times have you been a surrogate?"

Meaghan held up three fingers. "I enjoy it. It's not as bad as you would think. I just tell myself to go for it and things tend to have a happy ending."

By Wednesday I was feeling swamped at work. A great thing happened when Luke and Jason confirmed that they could help with setting up security in the other labs, but it would be a week before Jason's schedule would allow his time off for the trip to New Orleans, and New York was a no-brainer since that was where he and Luke both lived. They would work together to find people in both Houston and San Diego they could count on. We discussed logistics. I committed to Luke for his friends' New Year's wedding in Manhattan. I'd just have to work some at the clinic there, I told him.

Later in the afternoon, I called my mom to discuss her emotions about Dad. I also wanted her ideas for a Christmas gift for him, but she didn't answer.

Then I had a four o'clock Dream Fertility meeting with Sara Lance and Ben Trigg. When I made the merger announcement on the news, I'd said we were happy to share info, and now I had to make good on it, because that's what they claimed to want. I knew better and wondered if she would be a bulldog in person. I thought it best if our interactions occurred in the lab, and not my office or any other meeting or drawing rooms where patients might be.

I sat on a stool, but the two Dream Fertility embryologists declined to sit. Fanny joined us late. Introductions were made.

Embryologist Sara Lance. Pretty, sharp nose, and intelligent eyes.

Embryologist Ben Trigg. He looked very young, had a cowlick.

Polite smiles.

"Welcome," I said. "We are glad to have you today."

Sara started talking immediately. "We may not have the same stats you have, but we get many, many patients. Besides, we don't have the negative press that you do at Chicago Live Births. You know, sorry about the mix-up scandal.

"And I heard there's undesirable news focused on Belle, saying she was a scapegoat and—"

"She is a victim in the games of a mega-clinic," Ben said.

Fanny looked away, but I stood firm. "This might be one person's opinion. It's not true."

"Just watch the news," Sara said. "Two nights ago, on an aired interview, a clinic in Northern California said CLB's patient was being coerced and called the situation the worst nightmare of nightmares."

I winced. I knew what was going on. The plan was not for Dream Fertility to come for ideas and assistance in the fertility advancement; it was to degrade our clinic. Normally embryologists come to us wide-eyed and excited to learn and share. These eyes were fiery, so I was confused as to why they'd come. Putting us down would only take them so far.

I pulled up my iPad and gave them the stats on summoning patient cycles as the baseline, and how it favored success rates over the clinics using the doctors' planned availability. I'd performed this analysis after Violet had complained in our initial conversation. Now I gently dived in, and then built strength with numbers from our five clinics, comparing the IVF success rates over those where the five clinics utilized the doctors' schedules for the basis of procedures.

"Well, I'll be," Ben said. "You're attacking our method. We don't want to be on call all the time."

"Use it as you see fit. Just thought I'd show you. It's an example of how I can pool info from our five clinics to help the industry. There are more." I turned to click on another folder. At the time of the merger I had offered to help other clinics so we didn't seem an industry monopolizer; I was learning. Next time I would be less liberal.

"That's not a bad idea," Sara said, "if you're used to having the luxury of being around as long as you guys have. Besides, that is the way we've always done it. Why should we change?"

I left it dangling out there, hoping she'd see the contradiction. "I can show you some other data sets that might be useful."

Ben pointed his finger at me. "We'll watch and wait. Thanks for your time."

Fanny put both hands on her hips, and looked confused.

Ben motioned to Sara. "Come on, let's make like a tree and leave."

I thought of Tucker. I barely held back my laughter.

When Belle called around two the next afternoon, I told her I'd rather talk in person. I was miffed at myself for missing the news about the coercion comment that Sara Lance had brought up. I assigned Maple the task of poring over the media and keeping David and me informed of any references to the mix-up or anything about our clinics and labs.

Belle joined me in my office. It was a bluebird day, and the light coming through the windows gave the room a positive feel. Hopefully we would have a great talk.

Belle sat tall in an armchair. "My attorney's talking with the US Food and Drug Administration. I am upset and need to know just how you are governed and what rights I have."

She dangled her water bottle from one hand, and in the other she held a small bag of carrot chips, which she placed on her knee. A loose-fitting navy top with a pink garden print would soon be replaced with a blouse that would accentuate her belly bump.

"I just don't know how I am going to make it through this. I feel like everyone is staring at me because they know I'm the one who was wronged. I don't want to be a victim, but it's what it feels like." She began chewing on the corner of a fingernail until she realized what she was doing and jerked her hand out over the bag and selected a carrot.

"Belle, please, we want to help."

"You keep saying that. I'm in no mood for it. What does it mean? Help? You can't change the fact that there was a big screw-up. You can't change that these two babies are beating me up!" She brought the carrot midway to her mouth. "I'm so sorry. Let's focus on the surrogate. You've already met her. Can you tell me about her?" *Crunch. Chew. Chew.*

"Meaghan?"

"Yes."

"Her energy is radiant. She's all about health and good fortune, and through any crazy destiny or circumstance she winds up having your twins, you'll be glad she's the one."

"That's a relief. Is she about to start?"

"Yes, we're planning on an IVF transfer very soon. We'll find out about the results close to New Year's."

Crunch. Chew. Chew.

"You will like Meaghan Wilson."

There was a moment of reflection.

"Let's hope my blastocysts like her."

It didn't stop.

I was checking the board again in the lobby and asking Maple if there was any other blasphemous news on us when Janie dropped in. She looked glamorous, exceptionally so. She wore leopard print stilettos and tight black pants. A grey tunic draped over the feminine curves of her waist where she would one day be showing.

All the eyes in the waiting room seemed to size her up to see if she was a new patient or one with successful IVF results.

I pulled her through the lobby and into one of the green rooms. While she settled her bag and heavy coat, I had the thought that we should add security out front to verify patients and all new people coming in. That might make the already fragile IVF patients more timid; however, it could also suggest our strengths, proving our desire for total security and protection of their precious sperm and eggs.

"It's so fun being pregnant," she said and threw her head back.

"Yeah?"

"I can't wait for you, of all people, to have one."

"Yes! In good time." I patted her high five. "Sorry though, I don't have much time. I have a full plate."

She frowned.

"I'm sorry," I said. "How's it going with Harrison? Any word?" I could smell her berry lip gloss.

She blinked away the tears that had welled in her eyes.

"Julia," she said upon pulling herself together, "thanks for asking."

"Of course."

She tipped her head toward her stomach. "I'm kind of used to the thought of doing this alone, but other times it's nerve-racking. Like birthing class."

"Is that why you are here?" I asked.

"You know it. It would be dreadful to go alone."

Satisfied, I nodded to show that I was ready to help. "Then that's what we'll do.

"I'll go to as many classes as I can, and if there's a gap, we'll make Beth fill in. She's a natural anyway."

Janie got up.

We hugged, and I said, "You've got a right to ask your friends to step up."

"You need me for anything?"

I shook my head. "I got a handle on this."

"Are you sure? I've never seen you so skinny before."

"I'm pretty focused on work." I sighed. "Sometimes I forget to eat."

"I'm cooking for two, so if you'd like I could make enough for one more."

I ushered her into her heavy jacket and checked my phone all at the same time. Thoughts were simmering about Belle and the threat and the schedule I'd have for work. I hoped I could make her birthing classes. "That would be amazing. I could use some fresh cuisine. I really could."

"I just thought, if anyone could help with my stress level, Mom could." She laughed.

"Well, I feel the same. It's mind-blowing how well we can talk to each other."

I agreed. "Dad doesn't really want to sell the house, does he?" I asked. "One of these days he will be ready for sure, but I doubt it's now."

I cradled the phone and pulled on sweats and tied the purple cord at the waist and then wandered down the hall and into the living room. I began sorting and shifting through the towering piles on my desk while my mother talked.

"Uh-huh, yeah," I said when she told me about her new blown glass bowls.

I noticed the unfinished album of photographs of babies born through IVF from our lab, the present I was making for Jim for his holiday gift. I thumbed through the collection, half listening to my mother. "He's got a few sunspots we have to check out." When I didn't reply, she said something I didn't catch.

"What did you say?" She didn't answer.

"I didn't hear you," I said. "Sorry, I was thinking about work."

"It's about your dad, but we can talk another time. What's troubling you?"

I told her about the pressure I was feeling at work. "But I just came across an ancient-looking photo of an ultrasound, and the handwriting on the back looks like yours."

"That's not likely," she said.

"Did you leave a photograph here during your summer visit?"

She cleared her throat. "I thought you might want it for your book."

"This is a book of IVF success stories."

"Oh," she said quietly.

"Mom—"

"It's you. That's your ultrasound. When I carried you."

"Why did you leave it? Do you remember my story from the beach?" We hadn't talked about this since I got in trouble. "It's been years."

"I just thought you'd want it. I slipped it in some time ago."

Why would she leave it without saying anything? I grasped the image and felt my throat catch and my eyes burning. "It might make me cry."

She laughed. "I hope that's a good thing."

"Yes! I love you so much."

"You're the best. You're not even here and you're the best. Perfect timing."

"Thank you, Mom." My phone showed a call was coming in. "Sorry, I've got another call. Do you mind if I take it?"

"Absolutely not. I'll email some Christmas ideas for Dad."

I shifted onto the other call. It was Luke.

"It's a Thursday night, want to see me?" Luke said. He seemed to be in a jovial mood.

"Yes, of course." Everything was going so well. I could handle the career challenges with all this friend/family/boyfriend support.

"Let's meet at the Apple Store on North Michigan in a half hour."

Nineteen

FOR THE SECOND time that day I dressed for going out. This time I chose stretch cords and a cream-colored crocheted sweater and buried them under a long coat with shearling at the cuff and neck. I tried to fix my hair with a little Moroccan oil and then darted out the door to hail a cab.

Luke was standing outside the Apple Store when I arrived, pecking away at the keys on his phone.

Every person within view seemed to be streaming into the store, each destined for an iSomething. Luke probably owned one of everything. By the time I was close enough to call out he looked up.

I showed my excitement, all right. I lunged toward him.

He leaned in, my lips parted, and we kissed. The crisp air of the night seemed to warm instantly. I tasted slight peppermint, reached for the hair behind his neck, held, and finally let go.

"Thanks for coming," he said. "Let's go inside."

Barricades, erected since I'd last been inside, channeled shoppers to the store's interior. It seemed dangerous. What if something caught on fire?

On the way in Luke squeezed my hand. In his other hand, he held a briefcase.

When we entered the room, a man leaning on a table smiled at me.

"It's Jason," I said and waved.

"Yes, can you go visit with him for a minute?" Luke said. "I have something to do."

I watched Luke approach an Apple employee and begin chatting.

Despite the cool atmosphere, Jason was wearing a collared, short-sleeved shirt. Behind him the Roman numerals one through twelve had been affixed to the wall. But then the numbers began to spin around the walls of the white room. Most of the customers stopped talking and watched them.

"Jules," Jason said upon greeting me. "I appreciate you making it out for this."

"Of course." I lowered my voice. "What's happening?"

Jason tipped his head to the direction Luke had taken. "iTime. He's launching it with you."

I'd seen too many movies. At once I began to worry about the "with you" and what was expected of me and wondering why Luke hadn't warned me. "Umm, I don't have the first clue how to talk about technology," I said. "Why am I here?"

Jason must've read the fear in my eyes. "You have to know you inspired him, right?"

Placing my purse on the table, I flipped through the iTime pamphlets while Jason attended to the final guests seeking out the demonstration. The iTime, French Quarter edition, was a watch with a screen like a mini iPhone instead of a faceplate with numbers. The user could see people and interface with them through the screen.

"I'll go to Luke's left," Jason said, "and you take his right."

"I just want to run away," I said.

"Why?" Jason said. "You're a natural. Besides I've never seen you with anything but picture-perfect confidence."

"I'm fine talking about embryology, but not all this."

A bellow of jazz horns interrupted us. French Quarter sounds were in the house.

Luke moved in front of the crowd, most of whom were focused on the iTime prototype he wore on his wrist.

"Welcome, ladies and gentlemen," he said. "Welcome to a new age of time, connections through iTime." He paused. "Its beginnings stem from the timeless underworld."

Jason nudged me and nodded for me to stand beside Luke.

"Here's someone who inspired me," Luke said as I walked toward him, "while I was on a business trip in New Orleans. And now, after some major developments, collaboration, and innovation, you can seemingly jump to conversations in cities around the globe. Let's just say you can travel as far or stay as near"—he glanced at me—"as you desire. Welcome to iTime."

A circular display appeared on a large easel across from Luke, lighting the center of the wall. He raised his wrist and the iTime glowed, and then it focused on a man wearing a suit, behind him a flag of France. Luke's face simultaneously appeared across from the Frenchman on the easel in a three-foot diameter circle, with a gold border glowing. The image on the prototype watch was projected onto the easel.

The music faded and Luke began to converse in French with the business executive on the face of the prototype he wore on his wrist.

I guessed that they were discussing the Euro exchange rate, maybe making a virtual transaction. Luke demonstrated how he could use a finger to scroll onto another screen, an Internet browser showing a photo of the French National Football Team, then the French Alps, and then a listing of French exports. He scrolled back to the home screen.

"Merci" and "au revoir," he said and disconnected. He then explained the partnering of Apple and Omega.

I smiled after my introduction. Luckily I didn't have to speak.

"Where do we get one?" someone shouted.

"When?" asked someone else.

The jazz gave a triumphant return. Luke clapped his hands. The horns silenced. Omega and Apple emblems joined together on screens around the room. Luke was swarmed. At one point, Luke caught Jason's eyes and then waggled two fingers in my direction, conveying that Jason should walk me out.

Somehow I managed to keep myself under control, but I was irritable. It wasn't the Thursday night I'd expected. But maybe it was better. The big picture was I was somehow involved in a major tech event. And that was huge. I had high hopes this new product would fill a market need, thus gaining higher ground for Luke and Summit Enterprises.

And fine if he thought I needed Jason as my guardian to take me home. I'd use the time to ask Jason questions about lab security.

I waved to Luke, trying not to show my disappointment. He had obviously been developing this over time, and I just wondered where I was tied into it all. Watching me sleep in New Orleans? Maybe he wanted to hasten production so we could use it to stay in touch. I didn't know, but I wanted to talk to him about it. How long would he be?

Jason and I didn't talk about lab security. He answered my questions about the iTime because I had become a space case after Luke had started talking French.

"It's obviously built with coaxial technology," Jason said, "and the iTime watches will absorb environmental turbulences."

"Okay," I said over my shoulder as I unlocked my apartment door, "but why didn't he mention he was working on any of this to me?"

Jason looked past me into my living room. "Maybe he was not sure it would come together."

I gave him a sideways look and said, "I doubt it." Jason didn't follow me inside, so I said, "Your call. You got me safely home, but you can come in for a minute, if you'd like to warm up."

He entered and held up a finger. "I just have to say it smells like a beach in here. I don't remember that from last time. And I pay attention."

"Or maybe you're just used to a smelly guy's place."

"Touché." He held up his hands. "It's all I know. I promise."

"When did he learn French?"

Jason shrugged.

"You do have a decent sniffer," I said. "I recently bought an air freshener called 'sea wave.' I'm having a drink. You want one?"

He agreed and made himself comfortable on the couch. I took a moment to serve red wine.

"Where'd this come from?" Jason said, holding his goblet.

"My mom. She's into making glassware. I talked to her today about some of her new projects. Want to see?" I pulled up her website. There was a photo of her.

He looked back at me.

"We don't look alike. I know."

"But you're both really striking—"

He didn't finish the sentence.

"How's she doing?"

I finished my wine. How was she? I narrowed my eyes. He cared?

I told him about our conversation about the ultrasound photo that was once me. "I'm a cream-colored gummy bear in a universe of grey."

Even still when I was droning on a half hour later he said, "Your eyes are all glassy, Jules."

"It's just, it's perplexing that I had to be the one to bring it up."

Before I knew it I was telling him, staring into his coal eyes, and he was into it and listening.

"How?"

"I got grounded because I got caught in lies."

Later, after I'd told him about my mom's secret, he said, "Show me another picture. One with your dad. Do you look like him?"

He followed me to the hall to my bedroom. Three framed photos stood on a shelf in a small cutout in the wall. I pointed to the one left of center.

"You do resemble your dad."

"A little." Why was this interesting for him? I was starting to feel wobbly.

Jason began examining another photo. In it, Tucker was sitting on my lap at one of Amelie's soccer games, giving me a thumbs-up. "He's a cute kid. He reminds me of Heath. Big eyes. He's the one that dreams of crocodiles?"

"Yeah, most likely."

I sensed Jason close, closer, and I felt a brush across my back.

"Sorry, that was an accident."

But it wasn't to me, it was like nothing I'd ever felt. A shockwave down my spine. Fierce and hot.

I spun around.

His cheeks were in my hands, and I lifted off to kiss him.

Twenty

JASON SHOWED NO emotional response to the kiss. "No, really," he said, "that was an accident. I didn't mean to touch your back."

I stared at him, one hundred percent surprised.

"There's a toy microscope or something, and I didn't want to break it."

I followed his gaze to the plastic toy on the floor from Tucker's science kit. I'd left it out to remind myself to return it to him.

"I should go." Jason turned quickly away. "It's not your fau—"

"Shh! Hey! Huh?" I finally caught my breath. He looked like he fit here, in my apartment. "What was I thinking? I'm sorry. Yeah, you better go."

But I couldn't resist running after him. "What do we say?"

"You had too much to drink. He'll know. He's too smart to fool."

I covered my eyes with my hands.

"It's no big deal."

No big deal? How dare he. I was angry with myself, even though it *was* my fault.

"It's hardly mentionable."

"Yes, you're right." I started to believe. "Do you think you can slip it in between briefings on South America, prank calls, FETs, and whatever else you talk about?"

I felt gut-wrenching guilt for flirting with Jason. Was I that hurt and angry with Luke? And for what? Finding him really focused on his career tonight instead of me. One minute I felt obsessed with

Luke, the next he seemed like a brother. And now I was seducing Jason. Oh, dear.

"Anything else you want to add?" Jason said. "You're on a roll."

"That's all."

"May I remind you, little miss laboratory, it's ETFs?" Jason seemed to loosen up.

"Oh, what'd I say?"

"FETs. What's that?"

"Okay, mister self-control—I need some water." I ignored my scratchy throat. "FETs are frozen embryo transfers. It's when a frozen embryo is thawed and implanted into the uterus."

"I'm sure you are very good at your job," he said after a moment.

"Thank you. And if it's hardly mentionable, let's go that route."

"Good."

I couldn't help thinking how awkward being around both of them at the same time would be. Also, I was worried Luke would somehow know.

"He'll already be angry with me for being gone so long on a major evening like this." Jason pulled on his coat.

The next morning I had an are-you-serious conversation with myself: *Are you serious you went after your boyfriend's bodyguard? That's shameful. That's hot. Angel vs. Devil. Are you serious you were denied? Are you seriously this stressed out? Or are you seriously blaming it on stress?*

In the kitchen I pushed up my sleeves and used my Keurig coffee machine to make a vanilla latte. My body temperature shot up just thinking about Jason. I opened the freezer door and took out a handful of ice and dropped it into the mug. Blazing-hot coffee splashed out. While I was cleaning the spill, Luke called. The ring-tone made my heart race. I hadn't had enough time to process the night before. Would I sound as embarrassed as I felt? I retrieved my phone and knocked *Fertility and Sterility* and *Human Reproduction* journals off the counter. I picked them up as I answered hello.

"Julia, hi! The night got away from me. Will you forgive me?"

"I'm not mad. That was terrific—what you engineered. The iTime is clever. When are they going to hit the market?"

"Let's talk in person. Want to meet for breakfast?"

I cleared my chalky throat. "Sure, but what was it about New Orleans?" The smell of the frothy drink seemed overpowering.

"It all seemed to come together. I wanted the iTime quicker. I wanted to release it, and I envisioned you as the model for the advertising. You know, looking at your peaceful face in sleep."

I wanted to ask, why me? I tried to convey peacefulness, tried to will my body toward it, but my heart was beating fast and my mind was swirling. "How about I meet you downtown in the area of the Ledge?" I watched the beige creamy liquid empty into the sink. "You know the Willis Tower? I'm sure we can find something good near there."

"The Ledge? The place Janie mentioned the night we met?"

I turned on the faucet. "Yes, you're not afraid of heights, are you?"

"I'm not afraid of anything, except maybe guerilla warfare."

Meaghan Wilson called as I reached Willis Tower, formerly named the Sears Tower, the country's second tallest building. Without detailing anything that could be overheard and perceived as awk-ward, I confirmed on my calendar the dates and promised that I would be the embryologist on the case.

Meaghan told me that she was practicing some more intense breathing exercises to calm herself. She was wound up too, now. There'd been enough press over Belle's plight that people of every stratosphere were calling and writing. Someone had even offered to donate eggs to her. After, Belle vented to me in an email: "I don't do donations. I want biological!"

Familiar smells of city living: engine oil, waffles, and sour milk. I thanked her again. "Never had so much excitement around one of these in vitro things before. I'll do all I can."

"Thank you. See you a week from today."

At a coffee shop, I bought a bran muffin for me, chocolate croissant for Luke, and two orange juices, and then headed to the entrance of the Willis Tower. I hoped all the meds worked as they should to prepare Meaghan's body to accept Belle's embryos. I closed my eyes and said a silent prayer.

I entered the lobby close to the elevator bank. The line of people waiting to go up to the Ledge was unexpectedly long. Would we have time? I had an itch to see if Luke would come to the clinic and maybe make some calls while I worked on patient follow-up, other lab procedures, and again checked Fanny's charts. I sent Maple my plan and delegated a few extra tasks.

The line moved only two feet in twenty minutes. The chatty visitors in front, wearing matching track suits with a big yellow lemon and smiley faces, arms draping over each other, turned to me. One of them passed me a brochure.

"No thanks," I said. "I live here." Even still, I stuffed it into my coat pocket and then read a text from Beth: "Tucker and Amelie miss you. Puzzle is finished!"

Beyond the phone, Luke's running shoes appeared out of nowhere. I gave him the down-up. Jeans. Polo and Windstopper jacket, both black.

He nodded. "Good call on the food."

"Thanks, and also for coming." I stuffed the brochure in my pocket and then we hugged. "Seriously, about your iTime?"

Luke watched me watching him. "I like this face." He leaned into me. Traced his index finger below the curve of my chin. "The face of iTime. I'd like you to model for the first advertisement. Trump Chicago called Vanessa back and agreed to the photo shoot there. Isn't that great?"

"Who's Vanessa?"

His eyes crinkled at my jealous tone. "Ha!" We shuffled forward. I took a bite of the muffin, and he ate his pastry and downed the OJ. "Don't you want to know about presales? Production? The photo shoot?"

"Are there fireworks?"

"Fireworks. Now you're talking." Leaning over he teasingly tugged my ear.

"Vanessa," Luke said, "is simply coordinating for me. There is nothing that can tear us apart."

I caught my breath. "Umm, just say that last part on the Ledge."

We finished the food. Every few minutes Luke pulled me forward, and I had this nervous work-tug as the time dragged on. "This is taking forever. By now I could've walked up 103 flights to the Skydeck."

"Have you done it—gone out on the glass balcony? Does the wind up there move the building?"

I batted my eyes. "It's my first time."

"First time, sweets." I wasn't much for long kisses but when Luke put his lips on mine, it rocked my world. Luckily, everyone around us was from out of town—or so I thought.

Twenty One

"YOU CAN SEE *four* states," a woman who had just ridden the elevator down from the Ledge said to her husband.

"That was incredible," a teen said to his mother as they passed us. "I didn't think I could do it."

"Did you snap my picture when I was on the Ledge?" an older man said to his wife. "It's one for the books." He hoisted a souvenir bag onto his arm.

"It's nothing like where you work in San Francisco," said one executive to another. "What's that, thirty-nine stories? I almost lost my lunch."

Luke had listened, too. He shrugged and said, again, "What's the big deal?"

"Come on, it's kind of cool," I said. "You could just be sitting at home on the couch."

When we finally made it to the counter, Luke told me he had it covered. One could just make a date out of it, too, I thought.

"So, in all likelihood, this is no big deal for you, but I want to thank you for doing it with me. I've been kind of nervous ever since—" I stone-cold lost my train of thought, because I spotted Harrison, Janie's ex, and realized he was with Sara Lance, one of the two supervisors of Dream Fertility's Embryology Lab.

I had had it up to here with the likes of these two. And here they were together.

"What's wrong?" Luke followed my sight line. "Who're they?"

"The dregs of society. I'll fill you in later."

"Be calm, we'll pass them."

"They'll see us."

Before I knew it, they were walking right up to us, Sara leading the way. She stopped, and he bumped into her. Sara exchanged a look with Harrison, who didn't seem to recognize me. He stood waiting for an introduction.

I stuck out my hand, "Harrison, I'm Julia. I'm friends with a friend of yours."

He bounced up, straightening two inches or so. Sara acknowledged the stiffness.

"I'm Luke." He wore his glorious, charming smile. I thought we'd get through the sheer awkwardness, but Sara Lance killed it.

"Your clinic just had six more successful IVFs. News travels fast. But I'm curious: why would anyone use you after the mix-up in the lab? The new successes will probably always wonder, 'who are my parents?'"

"They use us because we're good."

Sara smirked. She gave Luke the once-over. "Sorry, we were the last people who could access the Ledge. The elevator's broken."

Finally, an announcement over the speaker said the elevator was out of service, "and if you want a refund or to buy tickets to use on a later date, feel free to come to the ticket counter."

Luke's face fell, presumably from my build-up. I elbowed him. "It's okay. We'll use them on another date."

"Bye, Julia." Harrison seemed to have been in a chess match the whole time we'd been standing there. "Give my best to Janie." He pulled out his phone and turned with a frown.

Where on earth had those two met?

"Toot-a-loo." Sara waved perfectly manicured diva-red nails.

I narrowed my eyes. "Our stats are not subject to public availability. We've had six positive pregnancies," I said, thinking aloud, "this week. If you count Cornelia, that's seven. How does she know?"

"You want to check Jason's handiwork?"

My face flushed at the mention of his name. He meant check the cameras, but I was instantly brought back to my apartment last night.

Luke didn't miss it this time. "What's wrong?"

I sat on a bench. When he fell in beside me, I sighed. Disdain filled my words. "I'm a loser."

"What are you talking about?"

I looked away, fingered my coat pocket seam, and then I braved it. "I kissed him."

"And?"

"Trust me. He wasn't you. Luke would've kissed me back."

He laughed hard. I joined in. The heat left my body.

"Forget about the broken elevator," he said. "Here are the tickets. You keep them. I will only forgive you about the Jason thing if you promise me it's us from here on out. And we do this Ledge thing together another time."

I nodded.

"Let's get a real breakfast, then go to your clinic. You've got to figure out who the snitch is."

"You're right, and you can work on the photo shoot." I winked.

Les Nomades generally booked weeks in advance, but Luke had pulled one super rabbit out of his hat. That evening, after I changed into a midnight blue dress, and Luke changed into khakis, tie, and a blazer, we took his SUV into the heart of town.

Although he paid attention to my directions, he must have detected the flatness in my voice.

"Are you okay?"

"Yes, just a bit deflated. I want some answers. For heaven's sake, I spent over four hours trying to find out how Sara Lance got the info from the clinic."

"I know."

He'd been right there, too, making calls from every floor I went to.

"Let's talk about Christmas," he said. "I know we'll be together for New Year's but what do you have planned for next week?"

"I'll be working a lot." I turned up the heat. "And I'll be spending time at Beth's. It's what I usually do. It's fun. In spring I take a trip to see my parents. What about you?"

"I usually spend it with my family. Everyone's in New York. It's easy"—he smiled—"if I'm not traveling."

Inside the restaurant, the intimate tables were set with enormous vases of freshly cut flowers: roses, lilies, sunflower-colored Gerberas, and others I didn't recognize.

A waiter was laying the last place setting onto the pressed white linen cloth. He looked up at the sound of us laughing and said, "Welcome."

We were seated at a corner table. "You'll warm up fast," the hostess said as she took our coats. The air smelled of flowers, salmon, sea salt, and honey. Near us an older gentleman told a story about letting go of his pilot's license in exchange for a dream to skipper his friend's boat in the Abacos, Bahamas. I knew it was a revered sailing destination.

Luke picked up the menu and asked how I felt about raw oysters on the half shell.

"You bet. Let's throw in the calamari too, if you like it."

The French cuisine all sounded pleasing; however, in the end we decided on the braised beef for our main course. "We might have too much," I said, "but then again it's been forever since we last ate."

Luke beamed an all-star smile. "Now what's on that precious mind of yours?"

"I could start out with a concern I have regarding another confidential patient."

I thanked the waiter for the buttery French white he'd recommended. We clinked our wine glasses.

After I took the first sip, he said, "Let's just say Patient Euphoria."

"Ha! She's anything but. Patient Euphoria is having a crazy time getting pregnant. She can't naturally, nor by IVF. Every time I recommend a donor for eggs for either her or a surrogate she practically has an all-out hissy fit. Now this is some kind of angst in her heart. She wants her own offspring."

"Can you blame her?"

I tried again. "If you were married and you couldn't conceive with your spouse, and she couldn't grow her own eggs, would you consider an egg donor?"

"Me? Ha, that's a loaded hypothetical. You want to have babies? With me?"

My face crimsoned. "I mean, why the hell not? But no, I really wanted to ask what someone outside my field thinks. I feel lucky that a woman donated an egg, and it was received and delivered by someone who got over the fact that I was not hers biologically. My mom wanted a child. I don't see why my patient can't get there. I'm just so afraid for Patient Euphoria."

"Can I draw a parallel? I see a look on your face every time I mention finance or technology. So, about your question, I can't speak with any background knowledge." He looked rather foggy and searching, but suddenly his eyes lit up. "But my mom might be someone you can talk to since she's got a friend who went through this after a car accident." He waved a hand. "Way back when this craze started."

"You mean advancement?" I laughed.

"Yes, exactly." He smiled. "Always good at math, since I can remember, so it was a natural path for me. But you . . . your career was pretty much an emotional decision, right?"

"That's true. But how I was conceived wasn't always something I was proud of. Once when I was a teenager, I was lying on the beach with a few girls and we were laughing at some joke. Then one of them, a girl named Brea, asked if it was *my* mom who had brought us lemonade earlier. I said yes. My mom had settled several feet away to give us some space. She was lying on a white towel, radiant in her new tangerine two-piece. I remember her skin was even darker than usual. Compared to me, she looked like she was born in the Mediterranean. I've always had ivory skin. She said it couldn't be my mom because she didn't look like me at all. 'She actually looks like me,' Brea said. She had lustrous dark hair, green eyes, and, of course, olive skin.

"I told Brea and the other girls my real parents were in a car accident and I was adopted. No one said anything. Brea looked at me with a very sad face, and, well, you get the picture. I could barely take it. I turned around and stared at the ocean. I heard all the girls whispering and saying how brave I was. Until my mom came over. She'd heard it all."

"Really? What did she say?" Luke asked.

"'I didn't adopt you.' I felt awful. Once in a homework assignment I wrote that I was adopted, but she didn't find out. Lying is like a disease, and I probably would have said it over and over again. I loved the attention. The girls looked at me with an intense admiration, as if I was so strong, enduring my parents dying and being adopted."

"Obviously your mom forgave you. What do you think is different about being adopted? I'm confused. Did she use a surrogate or did she carry a donor egg?"

"Adoption is just different. I can't explain it really. My mom carried a donor egg. She did, and I love her for it. But I still get this niggling feeling every time I hear the phrase 'biological mother.' Why is that?"

"Do you want to know who it is?"

Point blank. "Yes."

We both looked up. "Are you finished?" the waiter asked.

The plate contained only a few asparagus. "Sure, thanks. You can take it."

He quietly stacked our plates. "Can I offer you any of our desserts?"

Luke looked at me. "Sure we'll get dessert to go." To the waiter, "Chocolate anything."

"We have a chocolate tart and a flourless cake with a liquid ganache center."

"That's a no-brainer," Luke said. "The flourless cake."

After the waiter left, I returned Luke's gaze. Focused, gleaming.

Walking to his vehicle, our footsteps were tiny clicks among the sounds of the city cars. "At dinner, I did most of the talking. Sorry." I paused. "But let's talk about something else I've had on my mind. Like how you look, Luke, underneath the layers of business."

Inside my apartment, he flipped on the first light switch he came to. Once in the living room, he held up the dessert and said, "Take it all off." He swept his other hand the length of my body.

"What are you going to do?"

He laughed. "Unplug." He set the dessert on the end table.

He handled both of our phones. "Off."

Slipping the dress from my shoulders, he stared at me. He loosened his tie.

Several seconds passed.

"What, you're speechless?" I asked.

"Let's just say I can't get over how beautiful you are. I've never encountered someone so absolutely beautiful." He softly nuzzled below my chin and planted kisses on my bare neck, across my chest. "Or felt," he whispered.

My mind settled on a simple tune of an old favorite: "Fool in the Rain." "Good to see you're still hungry."

"Lie down, there."

I stretched on my back on top of the gray couch on top of the pillows.

His shirt came off, and I swallowed and stammered.

Grinning, he said, "Stay still or the chocolate wins."

He lowered the box of sweets, flipped it, and my belly rolled in ticklish laughter at the moist cake.

I rose and fell up and down sensuously. I closed my eyes.

Afterwards, he wiped my abdomen clean with his shirt. Then we were moving in unison. The kisses more like bites as we kept trying to find each other. It was messy love, not neat like perfect Hollywood. Part of me was hanging halfway off the couch, but I didn't care. I was panting, he was glistening like a maniac who'd raced up a mountain ahead of everyone else.

And we were both loud.

He closed his eyes and rolled off. "Thank you, Julia." That's all he said.

Sweet love and beddy-bye for him, but not for me. My mind was hotwired, and I didn't sleep.

I centered on the feeling of being spent. But half an hour later I thought about the future. Where would we live? Was this for real?

Rhythm and blues, I thought. He's steady, and I'm grappling with heavy eyelids and racing thoughts. I'd never really entertained knowing or being part of his family. What would Luke's mom be like? I wondered if he'd made up the friend who'd used a fertility specialist.

Twenty Two

ON SATURDAY AFTERNOON Beth and Tucker came by. Tucker darted straight for me when I opened the door. "It's been like forever," I said.

He hugged me at my knees. His butter-colored hair seemed to be growing out in the last few weeks.

"I don't like you, I love you."

"Thanks, Tucker. You know I feel the same. Come on in, I promised you Mario Tennis."

"It's a mushroom smash," cried Tucker when he spotted the Wii in my living room. He took up the remote. Beth had to wiggle off his lime puffy jacket.

He served a good one and then kept hitting the tennis ball through the floating shapes above the net. He collected eight rings in less than a minute. "Way to go, little guy. Keep it up. Do you want some spiced cider or something?"

He was too engaged to answer.

"Sure," Beth said. "He'll take some."

"What can I bring for Christmas Eve dinner?" I asked on the way to the kitchen.

"How about the vegetables?"

"Sounds good." I opened the cabinet and got out three mugs. "What are the others doing?"

Beth looked bemused. "Amelie begged Tommy to take her Christmas shopping."

I raised an eyebrow.

"No, not for a boy. Just her friends. It ought to be interesting what they come back with though."

We returned to the living room and there was another head on my couch. I expected maybe Amelie or Tommy, but Janie sat up, her gorgeous salon curls bouncing around her face. Her belly was becoming something for sure.

Beth moved my coffee table to a spot beneath the window so Tucker could have more room to play. I followed, setting the tray down. I offered Janie my cider.

"No thanks. It smells so good, but I'm full from pizza," she groaned. She got up to hug me.

"Me likey." Tucker began to jump up and down in his fever to win. "This game is so cool." The remote popped out of his hand and went flying. "I'm sorry, Ju-Ju."

"It's okay. It happens all the time." I passed it back.

"String a bomb," Tucker said to the television screen. "String a bomb, string a bomb."

The three of us stifled laughter, until Beth asked Janie, "Well, what happened with Harrison?"

"I . . . uh, took him back. I really, really like him. Things are good right now." Her voice trailed off as she watched the ball Tucker hit go back and forth. The opponent was a dragon and three Venus fly traps.

I laughed. "You're cracking me up. In other words, no tennis match."

"Yeah," Janie patted her tight baby ball. Her eyes slit in wonder. "I can handle this much."

Beth blew on her steaming mug. The scent of cinnamon and cardamom wafted around us.

I was about to go back for biscotti or something sweet, when Beth said, "You can handle a baby? But not another disappearance by dad—"

"Precisely."

"For the love of God, woman, what was his explanation for leaving you in the first place?" Beth asked.

I had to hand it to her; she was getting after it tonight.

Little guy turned from the game. "What're you guys talking about?"

"Stuff you wouldn't understand." Beth said.

"Try me."

Now I was rolling in fits of laughter. Kids these days.

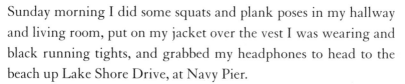

Sunday morning I did some squats and plank poses in my hallway and living room, put on my jacket over the vest I was wearing and black running tights, and grabbed my headphones to head to the beach up Lake Shore Drive, at Navy Pier.

My eyes roved Lake Michigan as I was running alongside it, in the sand.

A chop on the water as it stretched as far as I could see. A Spotted Sandpiper spun in the sky above. Three people walking astride toward me moved into single file to pass. Traffic to my left, but it was tuned out. The Violent Femmes shouted in my ear. I ran on.

The sun was beginning to sharpen. I picked out a target ahead on the beach, a barely recognizable shape, but I knew it to be the lone white chair, forgotten. As I neared it, I made an arc, adding steps to my run to burn as many calories as possible before the holidays.

Through the fuzzy glare of the sun I saw someone I recognized. I pulled the headphones from over my ears.

"Hey Julia," Fanny said. "Sorry, I followed you. I have to talk right now." She was huffing a bit. "Not used to running so fast. I'm cramping up in my stomach," she said.

Now there was something new. She always acted so tough.

"I was heading to your place when I saw you leave." She shrugged, flipped her hair, the blond waves falling perfectly into place again. "I tried to catch up, but you're fast."

"Okay, what's going on?"

"I didn't want to tell you while you were dealing with Belle's surrogate—"

Uh-oh.

"Another clinic offered me a position, double the pay. I'm taking it. You would do the same thing, right?" Her hands gravitated to her waist. Confrontational.

"Well, I guess so," and I forced myself to uncross my arms. I painted on a happy face. "Where are you going?"

"DF." Stoic.

"Oh, Dream Fertility needs help? I wasn't aware of that." My voice was so polite.

"They didn't but—" She seemed nervous; however, her pride won out. She knew something I didn't. "Sara Lance will train me before her maternity leave."

"Hold on. Seriously?" I said.

"She's been with the same guy forever, probably getting married."

I unzipped my jacket. "No, I didn't know. Sara Lance will be lucky to have you. You've really been working hard at CLB after the merger, and I hope it works out for you."

Her face brightened.

As her hands were breaking the hold on her hips, falling down, shoulders loosening, I said, "I'm a bit winded. Maybe we should walk a few blocks together?"

She nodded.

"Do you want to have children someday, Fanny?"

"Yes, it's my dream."

Authentic.

"I hope you do. So, who's this guy Sara's been with? I saw her with an actor the other day, at the Ledge."

"You did the Ledge?" she marveled. "I'm too chicken."

"The elevator broke, so I have a ticket somewhere. Sometime it's going to happen. I think his name was Harrison?"

"Yes, he's a hunk, isn't he?"

I knew it.

⊘

When I got home, I searched for the Dream Fertility website. The site was ordinary, nothing great. I was about to close the page when a pop-up ad appeared for the clinic: a baby in a palm. The words below the newborn: "We are on the road with you when you don't know where to turn. All the way to the trip home, safe delivery, and happy parenting."

It made me feel ill. My brain struggled to keep up. I sat there and thought about the past two months. Finally, I climbed out of the chair and headed to the shower.

After I cleaned up, I checked email and found one from Luke. He presented some ideas about the photo shoot. He wrote, "Vanessa has a couple of dress options, and please wear those earrings I like, too."

I rarely wore earrings, so I had no idea what he was talking about.

⊘

The morning after Christmas dawned with that holiday lull and serene feeling. I was slower getting ready for work and enjoyed the still air and bright sunlight when I boarded and disembarked the train. A few times on the way to the office I touched the sleek, new dangling earrings Luke had given me from top to bottom.

The package had arrived Christmas Eve, directly from Colombia. The contents were gorgeous. On each one there were four large emeralds in a vertical row, and individually shaped as a step-cut trapezoid. I fell for them instantly.

There were only a few things I had to do to transition Fanny's patients, and then I had a few more preparatory tasks so I could actually pull off New Year's in the Big Apple.

After I met with two of Fanny's patients to discuss transition and how we'd meet their needs, I ordered new supplies for the lab.

It was just after lunch when David and I crossed paths in the hallway between our offices. We walked to David's door and into his office to discuss Fanny. The heating element rattled, but there was something else. Bubbling, gurgling sounds from a spit-shined glass fish tank. Three blue fish with wispy tails circled comically.

"It's a Christmas present from Susanna." Then his voice turned to mild agitation: "I think they want to know all about us. And the best way they saw was to hire Fanny McCloud."

"Yes—however, I think it's probably best for us in the long run. Let's promote Susanna and have her post job listings for two new staff embryologists. Maybe even get a consultant to train her in management plus assist with overall quality control at the same time."

"Good, because I don't have time to train her," he said.

There was a fast rapping sound, and Jason walked through the door of David's office.

Twenty Three

"THE WOMAN AT the front desk told me where to find you."
Jason looked at me with even more intensity than usual. His coal
eyes sent chills up my spine.

"A security breach triggered my cell."

"Where?" David and I said at the same time.

"San Diego. The egg donor department."

In seconds I refreshed my concept of the San Diego clinic. David
had been there. He met Carlee O'Keeffe, who was kin to Georgia
O'Keeffe, the famous painter. Carlee was intelligent. And David
also said something about the prints of the Georgia paintings making it the brightest, cheeriest clinic he'd been to. Like clockwork,
their staff sent in the stats on embryo viability and birth success
rates. That was it.

"What if it's actually a patient who's culpable?" David demanded.
"A failed IVF or two and that's all it takes for someone to lose control and come after us."

"Seems like it would create more pain," I countered.

"Jealousy, emotional stress, bank account drained. Think about
it. There's a million reasons, Julia, why someone could turn if it
didn't work out."

"I guess, I've never thought of it that way."

Jason listened to us, and the longer we went on the more he
looked perplexed. "This is not my world. But I have boosted security and talked to the city police."

We both stared at him. I cleared hair away from my eyes. "Oh, yes, sorry. Go on."

"There was a break-in. By a kid, like eighteen, who worked at a dojo by the beach. Very beefy, and he was wary of the police and guarded. Said he thought he could sell them to his family down in Mexico. He had been smart enough to make it past the downstairs cameras, but the hidden camera near the door to the donor department put an end to his plan. He's being held for questioning. Also, he's served a little jail time." Jason attempted a smile. "I found it on the police blotter before they even checked."

I looked at him sideways. "Thanks, but aren't you supposed to be in Colombia?"

"I've got work here." Meaning Chicago. "I thought I'd come by instead of calling."

David studied both of us but said nothing.

My mind leapt back to the embryo email. "Remember that email signed 'The Embryo Clinic'? Remember the threat? It was something about look out for eggs being stolen from the main clinic. San Diego is not the main clinic."

"If you lived in the area you might think it was," Jason suggested.

"Maybe. Remember they also said they didn't mean us any harm. But it's hard to sort out. I don't get it. Who would come after us?"

Jason glanced at his watch. "I'll keep you up to date on this. Regardless, arm the security systems and be careful. Watch your video monitors like a hawk."

When Jason was gone, I threw up my hands. "The theft in San Diego is so strange. Too strange to be a coincidence. I think the Embryo did this."

Almost too calmly, David swept a net through the top of the tank. The fish swam deeper. "Can I cut and run?"

My mind ticked away as I slipped down the hall to my office; Jim would stop by for a visit soon. I hadn't yet signed the card that went with the photo album I'd finally completed, his departing gift. And yes, Jason could've called.

I pushed the door to my office open. Jason was sitting in one of my chairs.

"I'm just worried about you, is all."

It felt like a tickle on my heart, until he said, "It's simple. I'm here to work on some pressing things for the photo shoot for the iTime. Luke wanted me to check on you anyway, and here's a brief description for the required brief. The place that was chosen is the Trump International Hotel and Tower Chicago. Okay?"

I took the document.

"You'll have fun with it. I know you will."

Just a man doing his job.

I returned Jason's gaze and then bent quickly to scribble the thank you to Jim for all his teachings, just as he breezed into the office. He'd lost weight, but I saw the color in his cheeks looked healthy.

"You look great," I told him.

"Thanks."

Once Jason left in his stealthy fashion for a second time, Jim added, "You look great, too." He sat, happily watching me behind my desk. "No gray hairs! Despite the pending resolution for Belle and Theodore Harting. Will it be a family or not? I know it's got to be gut-wrenching for you."

I nodded then recounted the news about Fanny. Something about her was eating at me. I couldn't put my finger on it. I still felt guilty about being with Luke in New Orleans when the mix-up happened, but that was about me and—

Jim snapped his fingers. "I've a brilliant idea. Why don't you get that employee of yours to find out things for you at Dream Fertility? Infiltrate them." For a second he sported a devil smile.

"Fanny? Right. Offer her triple and still have to put up with her?" I shrugged. "And at that point we'd be playing their games.

It's easy for you to joke around." I laughed. "You only report to Diana these days."

"Yep, and that's a major downer," he teased. "I do miss this place."

My phone beeped. It was Maple asking if I could review Susanna's new hire applicant pile. "Only if it's under a dozen," I answered. "Could you email them?"

When I focused again on Jim, I pulled out the card and the book.

"Good thing for all of these people that you had a vision. Here's evidence of your work. Proof in the pudding."

"I love that line." He was eyeballing images of ultrasounds and the corresponding newborn pics, some black-and-white newsprint tear-sheets, others family holiday greeting cards with fabulous messages like, "Aren't we the lucky ones? Three cheers for a Happy New Year's." This from the parents of a set of triplets, dressed in matching red and white onesies.

In the dusky light coming in the window, I saw a large smile on Jim's face. How lucky he was without the operational and growth challenges. "Congratulations on what you've achieved," I said. "You deserve so much more."

He rubbed his throat, snapped the book closed, and stood up. He tried to tuck it under his arm, but the book was too thick. "Thanks for the best present. Aww, Julia—good luck."

I was tearing up and had to turn away.

On my train ride home I reviewed the applicant emails Susanna had forwarded to me. Earlier in the day David and I had promoted Susanna to executive staff trainer and Tia to director of fundraising. They were thrilled.

Susanna had already narrowed the search to a handful of embryologists from the nearby university.

I closed the applicant emails and put away my iPad. As I took the elevator to my apartment I had a sense of things coming together for a brief moment. Tonight it would be enjoyed by candlelight, not with Luke but with Tucker.

Beth hugged me, and then she ran out to grab a bite with Tommy.

"Tucker, follow me." In the kitchen I pulled out a wedge of Brie and prepared it with a train of raspberries, blackberries, and blueberries, his favorite.

Around a full mouth he asked, "Got any more?"

After we ate, I took him to the living room, where I danced with him in my arms to a Dave Matthews song called "Everyday." "You're heavy," I told him.

"No, I'm not. You can do it." We twirled on the white flokati rug until I was dizzy from the spinning.

"Again, again!" Tucker shouted.

"Even the petri dishes will weigh a ton tomorrow. My arms are gonna be so sore."

Later, Garfield and Odie helped Tucker slip closer to dreamland. As I closed the book, Tucker asked, "It's okay with my mom I sleep over?"

"Sure, she said it was fine."

As we lay together in the bedroom I told Tucker stories. The last one was about Tanya and her twins that would one day be born.

"On planet Earth?"

"Yep." I laughed. "Right here. In six months or so."

"What are their names?"

"Heckle and Jeckle." The talking magpies.

Tucker laughed so hard he truly wet his pants.

⊘

Later in the week I took off work early to hang out with Sam. She had two days off work and wanted to spend an evening with me at Nouveau, a spa. She somehow managed to snag the last two spaces of the day.

As I moved down Michigan toward the spa, I kept feeling like someone was following me or watching me. I'd whip my head around every now and then, but everyone I could see seemed in their own space or wrapped up in a conversation with someone else.

I began to wonder if I was getting a little schizo again, because tomorrow was Tanya's visit and the very next day I was leaving for New York. In three days' time, we'd hear about Belle's surrogate.

I found Nouveau, a little place tucked into a breezy space on East Walton. Sam said it was advertised as an "oasis of tranquility." That was fine with me.

Sliding into the leather chair, I rolled up the bottoms of the black yoga pants I was wearing. Sam came in from another room, wearing a tiara. I laughed.

"Hi, love." She hugged me tightly.

"Nice hat." I submerged my feet into the hot water. The warmth shot through my toes and began relaxing my tight calves.

While Sam filled me in on why she was visiting, I wondered about the conversation I had with Jim about Dream Fertility.

I wondered where Harrison and Sara met. At the play? She watched him onstage and she fell in love and manipulated her way into his life.

"Earth to Julia," said Sam. "What color?"

"You pick. Something good for my extra pale wintertime skin."

"Well, what are you wearing to the wedding you're going to with Luke?"

"Red."

"Oh, Racy, I knew it. Take this, Pamplona Purple."

"Great idea."

Janie had still been in decent spirits after I'd told her about Sara, which I had to do since Fanny told me about Harrison and Sara. When Janie talked to him, he had sworn he hadn't cheated on her, that he and Sara got together after. That didn't jive with what Fanny said though, because she had said they had been together a long time.

"There's a competing Chicago clinic I'm worried about," I said. "It's a long shot, but have you heard of a Sara Lance?"

Sam dunked her feet into the swirly, bright blue water. "Nope."

"What's your take on using donor eggs if regular IVF doesn't generate embryos?"

"Egg donor and biological father's sperm?"

"Yes. Like me." I'd told her when we were in school. "Should I use it to help the situation at work?"

"Why? What's making you nervous?"

"My patient is freaking out about using a donor. Would it help if I told her I came from an egg donor? And I explained that I feel like a part of both my mom and my dad when it comes down to it. She did deliver me. And want me, ya know?"

The spa beautician put paraffin on my feet. I felt trapped, but I tried to enjoy it.

"So you want me to help you solve this?" Sam said.

I remembered that at one point Sam had wanted to be a spy. "Yes, in your spare time."

"Ha! There ain't any of that."

"How about now?" I didn't bring up that I had felt as if I was being followed; she'd have a heyday with that one. "I know it's complicated. The mix-up, the Embryo Clinic email, and now a break-in—"

"Do you know about these other people at the competing clinic? It's a team of two, right? How'd they get into the field? Rise in their careers? It's all about motivations."

"Oh, darn. I don't know anything about Sara Lance, really, 'cept what I told you. She could be carrying a baby whose male genetics are the same as Janie's baby. This guy Harrison Bradner is such bad news."

I explained Janie's fiasco. I was still at a loss.

"I'm speechless. I've met Janie. She's sweet as cherry pie."

"Another Southern saying, please—"

"I reckon you better tell me about the other woman."

"Huh?"

The spa beautician moved my feet as easily as if I were a marionette. She dried them off so she could paint my toes.

Sam cleared her throat and gratefully accepted a glass of water from her gal. She turned to me. "The other woman who runs Dream Fertility."

"Oh, it's actually a man."

"Who is it?"

"Ben Trigg."

"What's his ticket?"

"I have no dirt on him."

"Get some."

The next morning, I dressed quickly and headed to CLB, where I was met by Tanya.

"I know we don't have an appointment for real," she said, "but I need to talk to you about Belle."

"Sure, what's new?" I hastened her to follow me past the atrium to a patient room.

As we entered, she said, "She's calling me about their movements all the time."

I took a seat after she did and gazed back into her almond-shaped eyes, which reminded me of Beth's. "Well, that's good, right? Sounds okay to me. The ultrasounds show two healthy heartbeats and perfect sharing from the placenta."

A deep breath. "I know, but I can't help—" tears began to well in the corners of her eyes, making the almond shapes nearly go flat.

I passed her a tissue.

"It's just, I can't believe she's doing all this for us."

I waited. "It's merciful."

Tanya closed her eyes, and then opened them. "Here's a what-if. What if I consider giving her one of the babies? I don't have to have twins. I only wanted one in the first place!"

Twenty Four

TANYA HAD THE face of a child, so it was a bit surreal to discuss the fact that she would soon have children, let alone that she was contemplating giving one of them away, that she would be separating twins at birth.

This wasn't my most dumbfounded moment, but it was close.

She crossed her legs. She was quite petite; I'd nearly forgotten her tiny size. Twins might've been harder for her to carry, so that probably entered her mind time and again when she saw Belle, who was tall.

I thanked her for coming in with her concerns. "Let's play this out and see what happens in a few days. That's not far off."

My first instinct was to say "no way" about rearing the twins apart. However, there was a published finding from the Minnesota Twin Family Study that followed twins who were separated at birth and reared in different families. I'd need to review it, but I recalled the quick synopsis was that Thomas Bouchard concluded co-twins were similar due to genes and not environment. But it was crazy to think that Tanya was considering raising one twin and letting Belle adopt and raise the other.

What in the world was I supposed to say? The room remained quiet for a beat. "Have you mentioned this to Belle? Have you and your husband discussed it?"

"Neither," she answered. "I wanted your opinion first."

I was sucking on my third cough drop when I landed at LaGuardia on New Year's Eve. I felt like a menthol doll, but the drops helped to ease the soreness in my throat. Still, I unwrapped a fourth one. I was bummed that I was feeling poorly the day before Luke and I were supposed to attend a wedding.

I wasn't feeling like making any kind of spark happen right away with Luke, but it would have been nice to wrap my arms around him right then. I checked my phone as I followed the masses to the baggage claim area. Nothing from him.

After I retrieved my belongings, I wheeled my suitcase out to the curb and looked up and down for his black Beemer, but it was nowhere to be found. I checked the phone again.

I pulled out my tissues, wiped my raw nose, and then dropped the Kleenex into a garbage can. I turned, and Jason was standing beside me. He quickly said hello and took my bag.

"You again," I said and laughed. But in his eyes I noticed a change, his usual wit in absentia.

"Luke's delayed." He raised his sunglasses from where they hung around his neck. "You don't sound good."

"It's just a cold." I sniffed. "I've been working too much."

"I'm right over here."

I followed him to Luke's Beemer, which was hidden from view behind a shuttle van. "How are you?"

He ignored me the first time, and after he deposited my bag into the trunk of Luke's car, he mumbled to himself. "Who cares?"

"I do. Everything okay?" I couldn't help but glance at him. "Something must be wrong."

His eyes seemed to glow through the sunglasses. "Whatever you say."

"Hey, I'm sorry. I've never seen you mad before." He was usually calmer than ten cucumbers.

"Well, my day's sucked."

"What happened?"

"I can't talk about it."

Stony silence.

I'd find out from Luke. There was probably trouble at the mine. But when we drove out the airport exit, Jason told me Luke wasn't coming back until the next day.

"What am I supposed to do?"

"Well, you don't have to figure it out. I've done it for you."

Again, silence.

What did he have in store? The music was some I liked—old Van Morrison. I nursed my cold and sat there wondering where we were going and how not to tick him off.

Jason drove up to the curb at the rink of the Rockefeller Center and said, "Luna, Luke's mother, will meet you at the Rock Center Café. From there you can get some skates."

"Ice skating?" With Luke's mother? I don't remember if I breathed or even closed the car door or waved goodbye.

Dressed in all winter white, and tall like Luke, with feathery caramel highlights peeking out from an ecru beret, she stood out. I couldn't have missed her if I tried. She looked familiar. I saw her first, which was helpful. I took a deep breath and then tapped her shoulder. "Hi, I'm Julia. You must be Mrs. Ashton."

"Call me Luna. What a pleasure." Sincere.

"Is this your favorite thing to do in the city?"

"Comes mighty close. My other prized spot is the High Line. It's an old train track above street level that has been converted to a park."

We walked together to the skate rental area. I noticed the skates Luna had were custom. It was warm inside the Rock Center, and she took off her gloves while we waited.

"I've heard of it. On the West Side?"

She nodded and smiled. "One day, darling, you should go there." She didn't add Luke anywhere in there. Was she protective? Was she looking at me funny?

"I just realized I think I've seen you at the New York Embryonic Center."

I felt my head nodding, and I was surprised. I figured it out; she did look familiar. "Yes, you're right. You were leaving. Now I remember."

"I knew it." Luna snapped her fingers and her charm bracelet shook on her wrist. One of the charms holding a photo caught my eye. "Is that your other son?"

I paid the clerk for size seven skates and handed over my boots.

"Ridge. Yes, Luke's younger brother."

"I started to say that they looked alike, but they don't. Ridge looks like you."

Her voice grew tender. "I agree. You don't have to skate if you don't feel up to it."

"The fresh air might help."

Then it was time to lace up the skates. The pair I'd rented was broken in, but my hands were cold and my nose was running. I struggled, and then I began to laugh, because Luna had made at least two laps around the ice rink.

She swirled in my direction and then stopped abruptly—and gracefully.

"You're good."

"I ought to be, as many business clients as I've entertained here."

She shrugged sweetly. "I enjoy it more now. You want me to give you some tips?"

Though I was having fun making the figure eights Luna taught me, the thought of something warm on my throat, maybe hot chocolate, brought me in from the cold. Luna skated while I stood in line. I sat on a bench near some others and blew on the steaming cup. A whistle blew and music came over the speakers, a Bing Crosby Christmas song.

Luna skated up, her soft complexion turned rosy. I was inspired by the fact that she was in her late fifties and didn't feel the need to cover any facial blemishes with foundation. The smattering of cute freckles across her nose made me smile on the inside.

Luna sat beside me and slipped her hands into the pockets of her white down jacket.

"Want some?" I held up my cup of hot chocolate.

"No, thank you."

I saw a window. I held the cup in both hands, and turned to face her. "Luke said you became interested in fertility science because a friend was in an accident. There have been so many recent changes in the industry. There are so many more opportunities now since frozen eggs remain viable infinitely after the initial freeze. It's time suspension; they don't age."

"I did have a friend who was in an accident. I thought Ellie should freeze her eggs. And I went with her a few times, and then I just somehow joined the board. Immediately, I considered becoming an egg donor. I'd just had Ridge and was feeling so magnanimous. Very high on life."

"Wow, sounds incredible." I meant the feeling. My mind started to race. And all of a sudden I realized it was Luke's mother who I was having this intimate conversation with. It both scared and exhilarated me.

Luna circled back about Ellie: "So the injuries from the car accident could've produced issues with her physically, possibly affecting her fertility. I helped her with her emotions. I do wish she'd had the benefit of vitrification that is available today—the flash freezing." She looked away and then back.

"Since I'd gotten to know Dr. Swan and the others at the clinic, I began to help with fundraisers and outreach with past IVF patients. It was easy and fun."

I stared out at the other skaters. A gentleman stopped to help a fallen girl, who had also lost her bright pink hat halfway across the rink.

"Do you mind if I ask how it went with your friend Ellie?" I finished off the hot chocolate.

A cloud of pain crossed her face. "Not well."

I remembered the last night I couldn't sleep like this. Luke and I referred to that time as "chocolate fest." I tried to replay the memory in my head, but with congestion, body ache, and headache, the moment didn't seem as good as I might've remembered. I was all alone in a hotel room, coughing with a scratchy throat.

I sat up and pulled on some of the slippers they offered guests. Bah! I wiped my nose. Retrieving my iPad, I fired up the Internet and wiped my nose again. A half hour of searching taught me a lot.

Colombian emeralds are said to be the rarest in the world because they are the only emeralds formed in host rock that is sedimentary, not igneous. The earthly tectonic movements occurring now and in the past, the formation of the Andes, produce these three scarce elements: beryllium, chromium, and vanadium. Found in liquids and gases, and when moved into the cracks of sedimentary rock, it cools and crystallizes, and is lastly perfected with a natural saline that reduces the iron and other impurities. Emeralds in the deepest mines of Colombia are stones like no other: the darkest crystalline green gems on earth.

The pinpoint on the map is the eastern edge of the Andes, a place between the Boyacá and Cundinamarca "departments." I studied Muzo because it seemed the most widely referenced. It was under a long-term lease from the government to a Colombian company.

"Muzo" was not just a name of the actual mine, but indeed described the quality and color of emeralds. In this case, the native meaning was "warm, grassy-green emerald, with hints of yellow." Over seventy-five percent of the Muzo population worked in the emerald niche. What did that mean? Precarious things.

Emeralds were at the center of the countrywide dispute. Heated and acrimonious, the civil war was among the guerillas and Lefty-activists, paramilitary Righty-activists, the drug ring, and the government. How would anyone know who was who?

And there was a very specific clash of weapons in the seventies that left two thousand dead. And always, smugglers were going after the rough emeralds, which were kept in safe houses until being shipped to areas of lesser danger.

With emerald value being what it was, no wonder there were those who tried to use it as the means to funnel crazy money in Colombia by "finding" and selling the gems illicitly "in order to fund their existences." It made me shiver.

I was eyeballing images of the town and the surrounding mountains, trying to imagine Luke there. It was probably lush green as far as he could see, when the misty clouds cleared out. Inside the mine, he probably saw just specks of light in the vast eternal darkness.

The gemstones extracted from such deep places, though, were in a word, legendary. With less iron in the emeralds, the Colombian gems dazzled an enhanced green hue. Set against black web backgrounds, they nearly glowed at me.

I leaned into the arm of the couch and wondered to what extent

Luke was involved. Having an understanding of his big personality and drive made me nervous for him.

My thoughts began to spin as I stared at the Colombian emerald earrings in my hand. All of a sudden I felt pressure in my head, like I was scuba diving and couldn't equalize.

I remembered that the gym was open twenty-four hours. With no regard for the fact that it was pushing eleven p.m., I pulled on yoga pants with a tank and the slippers I found in the room. If I sat in the steam room, I might be able to shake the fuzzy brain and sleep.

The gym door required the access card, which I had left in the room four floors up. Great.

After I visited the front desk for a new card, I slipped it through the access on the gym door. Inside the quiet gym I found the steam room and ended up leaving my music outside. I took a hand and smoothed the steam from the glass. I'd come to the gym partly to take my mind off Luke, but I couldn't stop worrying about him.

My mind returned to New Orleans. From Colombia herself, Maria Jose divulged her major suspicions about Fanny. I questioned whether I was satisfied with the B&T switch. Belle and Theo, Boyd and Tanya. I had not been able to come up with one good reason to fire Fanny; even if she didn't have anything to do with the switch, she didn't have a solid work ethic. Since the mix-up, I'd had a fuzzy brain over Luke.

Forcing the thoughts out, I stood and grabbed a towel. I felt alone.

Twenty Five

AND IT WAS a new year. Exactly eighteen hours later Luke was standing beside me in a tuxedo. He looked extremely blond, tan, and scrumptious.

"You're having fun?" he asked.

I nodded. "You?" He'd barely mentioned his trip, but then again we'd spent all of our hours together with the wedding party.

"I hope your cold goes away quickly." He angled his head. "Hey, maybe a strong drink will just take the edge off for you. Let's get one. I have to talk to you."

I wasn't expecting it here at Raoul's French restaurant at the wedding reception. Right now.

We parted the sea of bridesmaids—all wearing peacock-colored shift dresses—on our way to the bar. Holding fragrant stargazers and dainty callas, the ladies smelled of lilies. In tow behind Luke, I got a few extra smiles.

Above the bar hung a long mirror with burned edges that gave it a rustic elegance. Even the bar area offered up the restaurant's caramel aroma. While Luke shared a moment with another friend from Stanford, I eyed the art hanging above the mirror. The closest piece was a modern painting of a man on a seat sitting sideways, watching a monkey.

I had been given a playing card to hold in exchange for my coat. It was the four of clubs, totally unexciting. I flipped it over and over in one hand. Its edges were smooth and worn.

Luke leaned in. "I think you have to pass the tarot card reader upstairs to use the restroom."

I glanced warily at the wrought-iron spiral staircase.

We ordered cocktails, and then Luke whispered, "Something happened with the emerald mines. It's very bad, and I'm out. I have decided one more trip. That's all."

"Why one more? What happened?"

He twisted a strand of hair away from my eyes. My skin alerted to his touch.

"The risks are exorbitant—more than I bargained for." His eyes narrowed. "Besides, I love you too much."

Sanguine light and babies and beaches and other crazy visions were passing rapid-fire inside my head. "What?"

He grabbed my hand firmly, startling me. "Do you feel the same way for me? I need to know."

I'm sure my eyes were huge. I heard myself say, "Umm, really, yes."

Then he was talking to the bride and groom, Darla and Charlie, his voice less urgent: "Oh man, this is the end of one chapter of your lives, now for the next one together. What will it bring?"

Darla's maid of honor passed out small teal-colored bags of rice that was to be thrown when the newlyweds walked out of the restaurant. I got emotional and began to cry. "What's wrong with me?" I said to Luke when we were alone.

"You?" Luke pointed to himself. "Let's just say, I had a thought. I'm feeling loose too. Move to New York. You're good for me. There's a clinic here that you can work from."

I shifted my eyes from him. "Oh, so it's that easy?"

He pulled my chin back so that I was facing him again and then whisked me onto the small space set for dancing.

He was so serious.

I had to laugh. "If I moved here, you'd just stand me up over and over again. Remember last night? By the way, I enjoyed meeting your mom."

He smiled fondly

"When is the last trip?"

"There are stolen emeralds I have to get back."

My breath caught. I cinched my arms tighter around his neck.

"It's killing me. I don't want to tell you any more. I shouldn't."

I was supposed to appreciate him sharing that message? It unnerved me.

He spun me hard. I was lifted up to the sounds of Frank Sinatra.

The clinking of glasses stopped me from requesting another dance. It was the beginning of the champagne toast.

Even under the duress of the missing emeralds, Luke had mastered his speech. Darla, in her after-wedding attire, wore a black dress with a neckline like a choker, and her shoulders were bare. Charlie pulled her closer while Luke spoke. The gist was that they'd been friends forever, and the reason why they were so close was that Luke planned and Charlie executed.

My ears pricked. Sneaking off at ten years old . . . off to what?

While Luke was hugging both of them, I slipped out of the fray. I reached the front of Raoul's, took the iron rail, and began to climb. My footsteps grew louder, the din below becoming one noise.

"The power of cards is not in everyone."

I heard the gritty voice of the tarot card reader before I saw her.

"The magic is something not everyone can believe."

My skin prickled when she peered up at me

"Hi," I said.

"Hello, woman."

"I'm just going to the restroom." It was past her on the left.

"There's someone in there. You've got time to sit."

Before I knew it, I was drawn in.

She studied some cards and within a minute said, "Florida is important to you, yes?"

I smiled unwittingly. It didn't matter; she didn't look at me. While she studied the cards, I noticed her ivory scalp peeking through the part of her raven hair, which cascaded in all directions. One small braid kept her bangs out of her eyes. Someone came out of the restroom and walked past me.

The tarot reader said, "You two are lost lovers."

I smiled. "I need to hurry. He's probably wondering where I am."

"It's not someone downstairs."

"Oh?" I held her eyes in mine. She didn't blink.

I could hear someone coming up the stairs. I took the card meant for the coat check and waved bye.

Luke was excited to see me. He waved from across the room and lifted his chin slightly.

I tilted my head, feeling guilty for some reason.

He raised a glass for me.

Alone together later, Luke allowed the façade to fall. "Jason or Vanessa moved your things from the hotel to my place. Hope that was okay." He looked very tired. We took the elevator to his penthouse.

I listened to the whir as we ascended. "Fine by me. I'm grateful not to make another stop." I thought about the night. "Your friends are so nice. The camaraderie and atmosphere, it was amazing."

"Thanks." He opened the door to his place.

I stepped in first. "No, I'm serious. That's the kind of thing I hope to adapt to my dream clinic, which will be like a resort where people can make friends and not constantly feel the pressures of home, work, and tired relationships. Something genuine. I'll call it Hiatus."

He took my hand. "It would be cool for some people, like an escape."

"Yes." As we moved into his bedroom, I noticed my suitcase at the foot of the four-poster bed. I laughed a cough. "I like your style." We were both clumsy as we piled our clothes onto the floor.

So, we tried.

First I elbowed him in the eye. While he was trying to get up to fetch some ice, the bed sheet got twisted around his ankle and he tripped and fell onto the floor.

"Oof." I fell onto him.

When he looked at me with a crooked smile, I felt endearment. And it was funny, too. I swallowed and said, "Want me to bite your lip?"

He smirked. "And finish me off for good? No, really that's okay. I've got a meeting with a colleague tomorrow."

"Me too."

"Then I'll give you some courtesy, especially since you're not feeling well to begin with. It's been quite an end to the night." He sighed.

"Yeah, one for the books. Your eye okay?"

With the ice on his left eye, we moved into the living room and sat together on the couch. In the other eye I saw a little clouding. He lit candles, and the room began to fill with vanilla scent. I was right. There was emotion on his face, a slight frown.

"What?"

He took the bag off his eye. "I had Jason follow you. Just for your protection, based on some threats, although—" he drew out the word longer, "I hope they aren't serious—"

"You had Jason guarding me?" No wonder Jason seemed irritated with me. It wasn't necessary and was probably annoying to him.

I stared at Luke. Then I punched him on the shoulder.

"But I can stop it, obviously. It was for while I was in Colombia. Just in case."

"I doubt you'll keep a low profile, even if you do leave for"—I made air quotes—"Colombia." A pause. "Your ambition might take a dive if you did."

"Come here." The ice pack fell to the floor. I moved into the crook of his arm, while he lay back.

"Ah, that's more like it."

From the way he swallowed or the way he said my name, I knew what he was going to say before he said it.

"I'm so attracted to you."

He dangled his legs over the end of the couch, and he sighed a happy sigh.

"And I to you, Luke. I to you." The tarot reader was the one who was lost.

"I," and he flashed the number two with his fingers. He hugged me for the "you" part.

I remained snuggled against him until the call came in.

Twenty Six

WHEN I HEARD David's quivery voice, I knew it wasn't good. I walked down the hallway and put my cell on speaker.

"The embryos were not viable," he said. He then said he couldn't call sooner because he was taking calls from the rising media, answering questions at the clinic, and feeding support to both couples since their blood tests at four o'clock.

"This is a loss." I stared in complete disillusionment. In Luke's den, the shape of the plasma TV seemed to blur into the wall behind it. I turned when a candle went out. The sulfur scent hit my nose, smelling of old, musty books.

"I know. It's manure in the barnyard. Stinky shit."

"The worst," I said. I fell backward onto an armchair, a very uncomfortable one. "Do you know why?"

"No, I don't have an answer. The thaw went well, remember? Meaghan's body seemed receptive." A beat of silence. "Belle is ballooning with Tanya's twins, and her chance just went to zero!"

He was right.

"Let's talk tomorrow. I fly home after I meet with Swan."

I finally fell asleep a few hours later after an imaginary call with Belle; in my dreams she decided to run away with Tanya's twins. Tanya and Boyd in turn sued Advanced Fertility National.

"About time you woke up," Luke said, his hand on my shoulder. "Your cell is driving me crazy."

"Why didn't you wake me?" I pushed up and rolled out of bed. I knew I was late for Swan's meeting without even looking at the clock.

Luke's forehead was more crinkly than I recalled. "Want me to drop you by the office?" He pecked me on the cheek. "I can if you hurry up. I have to get in touch with reconnaissance in Colombia, so I need to make it to the office in less than a half hour."

I felt my heart rate drive faster. "It's doable."

"What's happening now?" Sage Swan met me at the glass double doors.

I told Swan that Susanna had hired three associates from Whole Fertility Care, in the heart of Chicago. They were in the process of moving their lab into the university and needed to downsize staff. "Other than that, nothing good."

The office where Swan led me was even more spacious than his room before. It held a new leather couch and matching chair, rectangular coffee table, and Western-style art. "My wife's from Billings. I had her gather a few pieces when she was back home last time. Otherwise this place might be totally austere. What do you think?"

"It's big, but I like the remodel." I took a seat in the leather chair, but it was mammoth, too, so I scooted forward and sat on the edge.

"They forced me into it." He winked. "My last couch was a

real antique, and it probably dated back to the time when fertility became a science."

That would be 1978, when Louise Brown, the first IVF baby, was delivered.

He laughed. "Or the beginning when Hans Spemann won the Nobel Prize for embryonic induction."

Everyone in my field knew of Spemann, the German embryologist who made discoveries on the early stage of prenatal development. Ovum, egg cell, plus spermatozoon equal zygote. From there it then develops into a multicellular embryo.

I couldn't help but grin.

Tasteful figurines of cowboys on horses, lariats, and horseshoes were arranged on the display shelves that lined one wall. "I like that sculpture best." I pointed to a bronze cowboy on a horse in motion. "It looks to be one of a kind. Sort of resembles the owner."

"Thanks!" He rubbed his chin.

"You asked why it didn't turn out for Belle? The embryos were very, very good after the thaw. Maybe Meaghan's uterine lining was inhospitable. For whatever reason the implantation failed. I hate it when that happens."

Swan was looking past me at certificates hanging on the wall. "I know, there's that disappointment, and you described how your receptionist felt like maybe she told the media too much."

"I think they were just bullying her. Maple's great, and she feels irresponsible for even talking to them about the sabotage in the first place—"

"I don't think she's harmed us."

I shrugged. "Me either. I think the competition is fierce, and I'm still struggling with an embryologist who used to work for us, and now—" My mind wandered.

"What keeps you up at night? What motivates you?" fired off Swan. "That's the kind of thing you need to find out from Belle and Tanya and their husbands. That's how you can get into their heads and figure it out. That's the immediate endgame. The other stuff we'll have to address eventually, since it's all a byproduct of growth."

I showed him my mother's ultrasound image when I went to get out my phone. I gave Sage Sam's number. "If you ever need extra help here, you could get in touch with my friend Sam Stone." I ran a hand through my curls. "Sam's intuitive. And I've known her forever, since school."

I told him how I had spoken with Sam and thought with the negative news it was time I let my past assist with Belle's hang-up. "My mother used a donor egg. I would like to encourage Belle to consider using a donor as an option, but the hormones and logic and reasoning are all at play. Again, I'll see if she would go the donor route, adoption, another surrogacy, or as many straight-up IVFs as she wants to try. Obviously once she delivers the twins."

"The realization hits, doesn't it?" Swan said, beads of perspiration gathering on his brow. "The enormous challenges and threats our merged clinics are facing. Thanks for sharing your personal story with me. And I do like the way you always look me in the eyes."

"Ha, my dad would buy you a drink for saying that."

"Let me guess. He was hardcore with regards to parenting."

"Very," I admitted.

Swan had twinkly eyes, which made it even easier to keep mine locked on his. "Anyway," he said, "you are for real. You'll help Belle. You will." His chin rested in the palm of his hand. "I'm drawn to your power, your connection to your infancy—the way you were drawn to your career as if by an elixir."

Hearing him say that was a good moment.

He examined the ultrasound image for a minute.

I laughed. "You know," I said, staring at it too, "it's nowhere near the stark images like today's ultrasound pictures."

"But I remember images like these."

"It seems ancient. When I first saw it, I called myself a cream-colored gummy bear in a universe of gray."

Sage flipped the picture over and stiffened. He looked graver than I could ever remember. "It's grand sometimes, it's like a lead balloon in others. A lot lately, it seems. I remember ultrasound pictures like these—"

"Wow, I'm going to miss my flight if I don't hurry."

Had I not been lacking focus from the cocktail hangover or high on adrenaline from the startling news about Belle's surrogate's blood test or rushing to catch the plane, I might've paid more attention to this man's demeanor that day.

﹡

From the time I left Swan's office to when I got to the airport lobby, I made a couple attempts to reach Belle. I didn't reach her, so I called Theo's cell.

"Hi, Julia," Theo said. "Yes, she cries a lot."

"I'm so sorry."

"But no, the babies are not in any harm. She's dedicated."

The admiration was there.

"And I have my eye on things."

My heart could crack.

﹡

Luke drove me to the airport himself and was on a call for the first part of it. Only partially did I understand the conversation about the missing emeralds. Intermittent Spanish did little to help me with the translation.

The sound of screeching tires on pavement broke over his voice as a Ford Expedition ran into our lane. I closed my eyes, but there was no impact. When I opened them I realized Luke was swerving onto the median like Jeff Gordon going into a race track curve. Wow.

Bright sunlight on icy roads did little to help the slide.

But he centered the Beemer. "Whew!" A sigh escaped Luke's lips. The near collision shocked me, and I took longer to recover.

"Crazy drivers. What's this world coming to?" Luke said.

About five miles later, he said, "So if you travel here more, it sounds like you could use an assistant."

I hadn't agreed to move, had I? With all the drinks on top of the cold symptoms, I couldn't say for sure. "Would I know what to do with one?"

"You would quickly learn to delegate."

"Really?" I stared out at a plane taking off in the near distance, close enough to hear the long thunder tunneling after it.

"Yes, I have just hired a fourth one."

I gave him the stare-down. I'd only heard about Vanessa; I had no idea he had other assistants. A lump rose in my throat. This was something small, but it was something I felt I should already know. "Any other words of wisdom?"

"No, but let's just say I'll find a way to get you one of the iTime prototypes. They will want you to wear it for the shoot." He pulled into the lane for unloading only.

"You know, Luke? Maybe it ends up that the iTime is even bigger than an emerald ETF."

He grinned broadly. "Let's just say, if it is, you'll get royalties."

"Let me remind you, I didn't do anything."

He stared down at my figure and then reached across to my chest. Soon he was massaging me in his hands. I grew dizzy for love. Simultaneously melting and lamenting about having to fly home and noticing my cold had dissipated and how good it could all feel if we just had more time.

Two nights later there was a knock at my door. I slipped the phone into the pocket of the spaghetti-spotted half-apron I was wearing. The aroma was rich and savory all the way to the front door.

When I opened it, there stood Beth and Tucker. His eager eyes danced.

"What's up, little guy?"

"See my new backpack?"

I checked it out. "Sure do."

He ran a straight line to the couch. His blond hair swished side to side in the back. With a whiz of his hand, the zipper opened the pack, revealing CDs and books. "For Heath!"

I couldn't make sense of it and looked to Beth.

"You said there was a little boy in New York who you wished he could meet. Well, it's all he's talking about."

My mind caught on. "Oh, Jason's nephew. I did tell you about him, didn't I?"

I went over to see the carnage of superheroes, villains, submarines, and dinos.

"One day I'll visit him!" The saying "bubbling with excitement" came to mind.

I looked from one to the other. "Want to talk about it over dinner?"

Beth rolled her shoulders back. "Don't see why not. Thanks."

As we walked to the kitchen, I got Beth's attention. "It's still early enough in New York." I smiled. "We could send Jason a message and see if they could talk?"

She looked relieved. "It's all he talks about."

"I promise, I only mentioned the kid once, one night when I was putting him to sleep at your place. Geez."

"Kids!"

I watched as the little guy climbed onto a stool in the kitchen. He swiveled back and forth and beat his feet on the underside of the counter, claiming it was music.

Before I had finished pouring the Chardonnay, Jason rang back. He called me "Jules" and said he'd go pick up Heath. We could Skype in thirty minutes' time. Jason's mood was more uplifting than the last time we'd spoken.

Beth was sipping wine and staring at a picture of Jason I had on my phone. When I turned to get bowls from the cabinet, she spun me back around. "You go by Jules with him? I remember Jason. Julia—he's hot!"

Luke was hotter, but I didn't say it. I turned away. "I'll get the pasta bowls. Grab the Parmesan, would you?"

My voice sounded scratchy.

I was not going to lose my head. Jason was only a friend.

Twenty Seven

BY THE NEXT evening I'd worked a full day, and it seemed like no matter how fast I went I was always at least twenty minutes behind schedule. The workday concluded with a conference call with the five heads of the merged clinics.

Afterwards, David said he was heading to the gun range. While I gathered my things to leave, I realized how everyone had offered good advice, supported our outreach to the patients and our continued efforts with the media. But it took nearly two hours, and I was craving sleep. How could David possibly fire a gun, let alone hit a target?

I must have talked myself out of sleep. When the cab pulled up in front of my apartment it was nine. I raced up the steps instead of taking the elevator, my heart beating rapidly when I threw open the door, completely obsessed by the idea of the twins being reared apart.

Throughout the day, I'd built research into a folder called "TPS" for "Tanya's Proposed Solution." I wanted the info handy to help guide her in her decision-making. I double-clicked on it. I didn't dare offer the articles to Belle, since she was recovering from the surrogacy news and likely couldn't fathom any option other than having biological offspring.

The file included mostly studies on identical twins, with the hereditarians arguing that even if heredity and environment shape development, differences in heredity are more critical than those of environment. A study on 600 pairs of identical twins had particularly interesting findings. It had run for twenty years from 1979. If identical twins were reared apart (and obviously didn't interact) then over time there shouldn't be much disparity in outward characteristics, for example personality and IQ scores, even if there was a wide gap in the environmental factors shaping their lives. But I found it odd that the identical twins who didn't exude a close resemblance in these traits—personality and IQ—were ruled out of that very study.

Most startling: the twins had to volunteer to come forward. And what about those who didn't know they had a twin out there or even those who knew about their twin status but were not outwardly similar enough? And there was little mention of fraternal twins, who would be even less outwardly similar.

For inspiration I pulled up the ultrasound from Belle's file, made a copy, and dropped it into the TPS file.

They were so cute. In the picture I extracted signs of fraternal-ness: Each baby was in her own sack. There was a membrane between them. Baby A was closest to the cervix. Baby A had grown. The amniotic sac looked good. Baby B was curled up. Their hearts recorded beats of 159 and 163 per minute.

The mindbender for me was that Belle and Theo would officially have to make an adoption. Would the governing service even approve it? And ultimately, who would get which baby?

It wasn't really twins being reared apart, I began to think. But then, there was no guarantee that they would raise the children this way.

Then I read another article, about a study, "Twins Reared Apart," a Minnesota study. I found what I was seeking: why the twins were split up.

I discovered that in most cases the reason in the past for twins being split up was due to illegitimacy, maternal death, and China's one-child policy.

The most common reason twins were split up today surprised

me. I had to read the paragraph twice: "Today, the new assisted reproductive technologies that may yield several babies, not just one, have caused some families to relinquish one or more of their multiple birth children; these families may lack the resources to properly care for them."

I knew all of this, but hadn't really speculated on families who have multiple children through IVF.

I closed the TPS file. With heavy eyes, I climbed into bed to watch *Game of Thrones*. I promised myself I'd only watch a few minutes, but I was riveted for over an hour. When I got up for water, I heard my phone ringing.

After a pleasant enough sorry-to-wake-you, Tanya said, "I'm heartbroken for Belle. I'm sorry for her." A pause. "Should I be worried?"

My dream came back vividly, the one where Belle took off and disappeared with the babies. I shook it off. "I talked to Theo earlier. He described her emotional roller coaster, but I think that's got to be part of it. I hope all is as well as it can be."

"The house next door to them is for sale. If we buy it, we can live next door. Raise the twins together."

Did Tanya have some direct line into my brain? I told her it was late. "Get some rest, and we'll talk soon."

A week later, Luke sent a dark SUV to get me for the photo shoot. Destination: Trump Hotel. The black box on the seat contained an iTime watch, which he'd promised, and I'd promised to wear.

In between the two seats sat a silver bucket of fresh fruit. I nibbled a grape and then tossed a raspberry into my mouth. I gazed out the window as we traveled over the Michigan Avenue Bridge. When I was done acting like it wasn't a big deal, I took the new watch out of the box.

Never mind that it was ultralight. Never mind that is was a tech-titan's dream. Never freaking mind that there were diamonds soldered in with filigree around the face. I pressed a tiny button on the right. The face glowed with the famous apple. Something about the illumination and the contrast reminded me of the Muzo mine website with floating, glowing emeralds.

We reached the Trump Hotel in the River North neighborhood. I thanked the driver.

Since I was wearing casual clothes, I would change into the dress that was waiting for me. Stealing another glance at the elegant watch, I noted that I had plenty of time.

I smelled gardenias in the lobby great room. Amber light seeped through the smooth glass windows, which rose twenty feet from the floor to the ceiling, allowing for marvelous panoramas of the city. Mostly I stared at the great vantage of the majestic Wrigley Clock Tower and the Tribune building.

I found the elevator to the private residences. The silence was powerful, and it made my heart quiver. I wished Luke were beside me. When I reached the condominium, on the ninety-second floor, there was nothing but endless sky all around.

A woman stood waiting at the enormous door to the deluxe suite.

She gazed at me, features softened by a look of docile satisfaction. "Come in. I gather you are Julia Holland."

"Yes, I am. And you must work for the photographer."

"Graham Sutton. I'm Jennifer."

I slipped off my boots so I wouldn't make heeled imprints on the elegant, animal-patterned charcoal-and-heather carpeting.

She looked at the iTime on my wrist. "Oh, can I see that?"

I struggled with the clasp, gave up and extended my arm for her to get a closer look.

Her eyes bounced from the watch to my eyes. "Are you ready for a direct change of plans?" She leaned toward me and appeared apprehensive.

I shrugged.

"There's no dress. It was a last-minute change."

"Okay, what will I be wearing? Vanessa didn't tell me."

"Sorry if this is awkward," Jennifer said. "They were supposed to tell you that there's no dress. You'll be in a Jacuzzi in a champagne bath. We have swimsuit options for you."

"A champagne what?"

Raspberries and grapes were forming a big bubble in my stomach. I stood there holding the iTime box, waiting.

"You've got to be kidding." Jason had told me he was setting this up.

"It's provocative, but you're perfect for it. Come over to the mirror and I'll create your Popsicle lips. It's a stain." She glanced over her shoulder. "Can you just imagine the seltzer water in the bath is champagne?"

"I'll do it," I said.

"Fabulous. I'll go tell them."

While I waited for them to get it all ready, I checked my email and found out that Maple had discovered nothing really good or bad on Ben Trigg. I hated dead ends.

"Well, we've got the set all ready for you," said Jennifer.

"Lucky for me." When Graham Sutton, the photographer, entered, I felt a welcome feeling in this place of glass. I showed him the iTime. We tried calling Luke with it, but there was no answer, and I didn't know anyone else with one who I could call.

"When Luke showed it to me, I was ready to jump on this campaign," he said.

We both stared at it until Jennifer questioned him on the location for my head-and-shoulder shots.

"On the sofa and the rug. Both are good. Then we'll do the Jacuzzi shoot."

The iTime registered 8:10 when I climbed off the grand sectional sofa. If I hadn't had to provide the smile I'd shown over and over, the soft sofa would've been an opportune spot to kick up my feet and catch another *Game of Thrones* episode.

As I dressed I replayed the myriad of poses and hair flips I'd done. Who was going to notice me with the Wrigley Clock towering behind me? Or would that radiate the time concept all the more? Had it turned out effective?

I hadn't had time to nibble from the small plates of buffalo, skirt steak, chocolate, and caramel truffles that had been delivered. After Graham and Jennifer thanked me, I responded with, "Good luck." I opened the door of the executive suite, took my champagne bottles, and moved into the hallway. I had to set the bottles down to tighten the clasps on the back of the emerald earrings. Doing so had become a habit, since I wore them every day.

When I saw Luna walking up the hall, I was both surprised and concerned.

Twenty Eight

"LUKE COUNTS ON you, doesn't he?" Luna said, hugging me.

I pushed back to look at her. "You're in Chicago. What's happening? Is Luke okay? Is everything all right?"

"Yes, yes. I could just tell my son felt guilty and bad for missing your shoot."

I ran a hand through my smooth hair. "Thanks, I think it was fun. Very different from what I regularly do. But I tried to stay true to myself and, I should also add, keep my job."

We stepped into the elevator. Unsure of the next move, I looked to her.

"I asked at the front desk; there's a terrace for dining," Luna said. I noticed her freckles. She took off her reading glasses. "We could eat here anyway. I perused the menu while I waited for them to tell me where to find you. It looks good to me."

"Let's do a different place, Luna, closer to my apartment by Navy Pier. I'm hungry and tired."

"Okay, we'll find something. And I hear there are fireworks there on many an occasion."

I threw on my jacket. "The word is—Chicago is crazy about fireworks, didn't you know?"

It was an easy decision to get a "cheezborger" from the little place John Belushi made famous. The tavern was hopping, so we could only be seated at a table in the middle of the hubbub, nowhere near the outside windows.

I told her about the large Jacuzzi, how I'd watched them pour in all the seltzer water but set up dozens of used champagne bottles around the base of the bath. "Corks were standing up across the bathroom floor. There were so many, they looked like little toy soldiers."

The waiter interrupted, and we ordered two cheeseburgers.

"So you talked to Luke?" I asked.

"I did. He's located the emeralds but says he doesn't have the first clue as to how they'll get them back. There's no canon of ethics there. It's frightening."

"You think he'll ever recover the gems?"

Her eyes narrowed. "I'm not sure." She sighed. "Actually, there's something I wanted to talk to you about. He's torn, and he told you this was the last time, but he might be gone again. I don't want you to get hurt."

All of a sudden the people at the table beside us jumped up; I nearly did too. There came the sound of huge pops, and both of us looked at each other. The fireworks then started in earnest.

Luna looked rattled.

"Want to go watch them?" I asked.

"Sorry, I'm feeling unwell."

"That's sudden. Are you okay?"

She nodded slightly; she seemed stricken with indecision and anxiety.

During another bout of pops, I worked through a bite of burger.

"Dear, your phone is ringing," Luna said. "Can you not hear it?"

I grabbed my leather bag. "I can't hear anything over the bang. Let me see who it is."

Another pop.

I dropped the phone, then picked it up. It was Swan. "Oh, sorry. Listen, I can't talk right now."

"Well, when you get a chance please give me a call—"

"That's best. We'll talk later because I can't really hear you." Swan would have to wait. "I'll try you in the morning, I'm sorry."

Something was said on the other end, but nothing I could decipher. I hung up.

I loved fireworks and had ever since I was little. I stood up to see them.

But Luna asked me to sit down. "With the tumult of Colombia and all," she said, "I just think you'd be better off to keep your focus on what's going on here."

I was dumbfounded.

"That's it." Pushing the plate away, I thought I'd had a rather strange night. "Listen, let's not discuss this any more. I know I can handle the danger of the emeralds, I can. Please, just let me figure it out."

A man near the window vacated his chair, and it was just enough to allow me a view out the tavern window. Mauve and gold first lit the sky, then dropped a trail of comets. Hundreds of them. The next was brilliant, brilliant green. It was enormous. Twice the size as before.

When I turned back Luna had faraway eyes, as if she were searching for something. After she insisted on paying I said, "I'd like to go outside, see the end of the show."

We weaved through the tables to the front, where we said our goodbyes. "We'll talk soon," she said.

She used the exact words I'd said to Meaghan and in a similar tone. Not dismissive, but as if she had run out of positive things to say.

I leaned back onto the wooden deck rail and watched eighteen more minutes of triumphant explosions: shooting stars, large stars in the shape of a donut, flower shapes, rocket bursts. The colors of the fireworks reflected off the still water of Lake Michigan. The air smelled of gunpowder and gas grills.

That same night Swan also emailed me an article. He'd typed URGENT into the subject line.

I curled in and propped up between the pillows on my bed. I read on my iPad: Two twins that were separated at birth found each other, and realized it only after they were married. "And I believe," someone being interviewed for the article said, "the government will leave itself open to class actions in the future if it collaborates in keeping information of this kind from children who have been donor-conceived." I dropped my jaw. This must have been what Swan had wanted to talk to me about.

Maybe he thought that if Tanya's twins from the mix-up were separated, they could later in life, through a twist of fate, grow up and fall in love. But that would be crazy. Anyway, it should be an ephemeral thought for Swan once I filled him in. The twins were girls.

Calm for once, I drifted off to sleep.

During the course of the next morning I had a few more embryos to grade. The lab was quiet for once, and I sat staring into the microscope lens. It was day three for the embryo I was studying, and the cell development was not as advanced as I would've liked.

I initiated a meeting with Meaghan. I hadn't seen her since the news hit.

She came slowly into my office, wearing leggings with an oversized jellybean pattern and a striped shirt. I offered her a chair by the window. A small plastic bag crumpled as she took it out of her purse. Twisting a Twizzler, she raised it to her lips and took a nibble. She chewed slowly, thinking.

The room began to smell like strawberries and cream. When she extended the bag to me, I declined. She noticed the iTime on my wrist.

Just at the moment, Luke's face appeared in a thumbnail. I'd have to call him back when he and I could really talk, so I pressed the mute button.

I filled her in a little on the new technology.

All of a sudden she dropped the candy and put her head in her hands. She began to weep. She said, "I failed."

"Honey, I'm sorry. It's not a guarantee. You didn't fail, because it is not up to you." I now had her attention. "You did not fail."

Someone banged on my office door and then it opened. It was Maple. She had a wild look on her face.

"You're needed for ICSI," she said. "The nurse can't find anyone else." She was saying that I needed to perform single sperm injections into each egg, for a patient who'd already been through the retrieval process.

After I parted ways with Meaghan, I donned my scrubs quickly. Everything would have to wait: Swan's call, and by now Sam had called too. Even Luke. He probably left a message about locating the emeralds. I was saving the champagne to celebrate with him, certain that he could get them back.

Hurrying down the hall, I heard my name.

It was Ben Trigg.

Just what I didn't need right then—Dream Fertility, more like Nightmare Fertility. "I'll have to talk to you later. I have pressing matters."

"Wait!"

"No, please leave."

He bolted after me. "Dream Fertility doesn't want to go down." He tried to grab my wrist but I hooked my arms behind my back. These hands were fertility instruments.

"Who let you in here? You can't harass me."

"Sue me for it. My clinic's in trouble."

"Let's not be dramatic."

"Believe me. I'm in no mood for drama. Dispel with the attitude and listen."

"Well," I huffed, but I didn't know what to do. These people had been nothing but trouble since the day they showed up and Fanny made them leave, and it was the day of the mix-up. I had a flashback again to the conversation in the Houston airport rental car line, over Fanny's confusion about the location of Tanya's embryos.

"What kind of trouble?" I asked, but then I began to see. "You were here that day and switched the embryos. You sent the Embryo threat. You sabotaged our clinics."

"Now hold on—"

But I didn't really see clearly, so I was turning it all back on him. The sarcasm dripped, but at this point I had nothing to lose.

He held up a hand. "Just hold on."

I was close to escaping through the lab door, but he blocked my way. He was quick.

He shook a handful of papers at me. "Now here's a freakin' answer."

"You expect me to read that when you're waving it like a flag?"

"It's from Sara's office. You remember Sara Lance?"

I crossed my arms. "Of course I know who you're talking about. So?"

"This was in her charts, her patient files. Macabre notes, but I can show you later."

"Later? Show me now."

His eyes were glued to mine. "This, for starters."

I could only stare in bewilderment.

Twenty Nine

OUT OF NOWHERE I had this image of Luna in my head, like a hallucination. In it she was so young, beautiful and angelic looking as if she had just delivered a baby.

I was dizzy too. It was borderline creepy and very distracting.

"Are you okay?" Ben asked.

"Yes, I am." I struggled to get the image and the sensation to leave my mind and body. I blinked hard. "That's a travel manifest. From California?"

"That's right. It's Sara's. And another, for a guy named Harrison Bradner. They went to California together. You know him?"

I nodded.

Wind rattled the tops of the sweetgum trees outside.

Demetri passed by in the hallway and stopped. "I'll cover this ICSI," he said. "Maple said you have a full plate."

"Thank you."

"No worries." But as he moved past, he made big eyes behind Ben's back. Ben Trigg was someone we'd talked about in staff meetings. Demetri disappeared into the lab.

"How do you know Harrison?"

He sighed. "They're dating. Comes into the clinic frequently. He's an actor."

Also in Ben's cache was a printed copy of an email: the Embryo threat. "Tell me, how else I could have this? I uncovered it in Sara's drawer."

"That's enough." I put my hands up. "Have you ever heard of an attorney?"

"You need me. You need this proof."

It was all I could do to keep my mouth shut.

At Pierrot Gourmet on the Magnificent Mile there's every kind of pastry imaginable. The aroma of rich coffee beans softening and heating up permeates the place. It was my first time there, but I'd heard how good it was from Tia and Susanna.

I was dying for a latte, but I was waiting for Belle, who would show any minute. It was a Saturday, two days past the Ben Trigg visit, and I was still hopped up on adrenaline after my lunchtime workout at the gym.

I'd left Swan a couple of messages regarding his dropped call from the other night. I tried Sam too, but she hadn't answered. Where was everybody?

As if on cue, Sam FaceTimed me. I moved to a quiet corner of Pierrot's before answering.

"Hello, Sam."

"Hey, friend. Thank you. I'm taking a new job." She delivered the news with a satisfied look. "I'm working for Sage Swan."

I whooped. "Congratulations. I never thought he'd follow through. He's such a sage," I said.

Sam laughed and tossed her head back. I stared at her chin. "I already started the job. My favorite part is when I consult with patients on the embryo quality—what they look like and how they're developed. This is the trust. I had no relationships with patients before this. And now I'm recommending based on the quality of the embryos and what to put back. You've been doing this since we graduated! It's all such a risk, a ledge, a leap of faith." Her eyes sparkled. "And you? Is there anything new with you?"

"Not anything great like that." I told her about Dream Fertility and Ben getting in my face, alleging his partner was perhaps the saboteur of our clinics.

"I researched him for you."

"Oh?"

She cracked a smile. "He's from the Midwest, went to Cornell, had only two jobs—held in a steady way—since graduating from a program abroad. I called both people he worked for. They both suggested that he's not the glass-half-full guy, but they reckoned he was a great embryologist.

"So there's no blemish on him, but his partner Sara Lance is an old Hollywood vet. She was in a few B movies. A little risqué."

"Oh, yeah?" She did have that air about her. "Anything I would've seen?"

"With your personality and your schedule, Racy? I doubt it."

"Thanks."

"You've proven to be quite contrary to your nickname. Anyway, I remember you mentioned someone else at the spa. A guy."

"David Lazel?"

She shook her head. "Nope. He's not the one."

She was enjoying this. She and Swan would get along.

"Demetri Gibbons?"

"Who?"

"Never mind. You tell me who!"

"You told me his name was Harrison. And he wasn't hard to find. You won't believe this."

"Try me." No caffeine required. I was hooked.

"Harrison Edward Winchell—to be exact—had his first acting appearance in a small theater in San Diego. His parents raised him and his brother in Mission Beach. And what you might not know is he comes from a long line of Catholics who may be extremely against fertility measures."

"I wonder if either Sara or Janie knew?"

"I like the way you're thinking. Another important fact. His brother still lives less than two miles from where they grew up. Has a business near the beach. Seven employees work for him at this establishment. It's a dojo."

"Training martial arts?

She nodded.

Belle walked into the coffee shop. I waved, and she smiled and pointed to the line. "What do you want?" she called.

I mouthed, "Latte."

My eyes shifted back and forth between Sam on the screen and Belle. She was starting her second trimester, and the twins inside her were living the dream. Belle had a purse over her shoulder and both hands were hooked under the belly—hard to say if it was to support them or protect them.

Suddenly, an older artist type teetered sideways with his coffee right beside her. She slung her purse around in record speed to block her belly. The coffee spilled all over her purse.

I could hear her say, "It's okay."

The man apologized. She stepped forward and accepted a few napkins from someone else. She deflected the attention, never looking my way. She could use a new purse, though.

Sam continued the whole time, "These guys are especially hard, exercise most of the day. Google is a small wonder. I found eight Catholic churches within a half hour of Mission Beach. Guess how many dojos?"

"Umm, eight also?"

"More than fifty."

"What?"

She grinned.

"All right, just a smidge longer. My patient's here."

"I'm almost done," she said eagerly. "You had a break-in at the California clinic. Swan filled me in on that. One of the employees of the dojo matches the description Jason obtained. Connecting the dots?"

"Oh, Sam Stone, you are a genius."

The brain scale really tipped. Maybe Ben, Mr. Negative, was really Mr. On-To-Something, in this case.

Sam broke into my thoughts. "Think about it, Racy. What if it wasn't Ben that day with Sara? What if it was Harrison who was with Sara, pretending to be Ben? And either Harrison or both of them were doing something bad? Like playing around with embryos in the incubator?"

"I've seen him act," I said. "He's really marvelous."

"Precisely."

"Got to run."

"Let's talk in an hour or so. There's something else."

I agreed to call, tucked the phone into my bag, and joined Belle at the counter. "The baby bump is aptly named," I said. "Don't you think?"

She gave a partial hug. The firmness of her belly shouldn't have surprised me, but feeling it against me made me realize how surreal it all was.

"I get bumped all the time."

But my mind raced with how all these coffee shop patrons had no idea that Belle was pregnant with twins and would have to hand them over to someone else once they were born. "It's noisy here," I said. "Not private at all."

"I know." She blew her bangs out of her face. "It's 20 degrees outside and like 120 in here."

"We could walk."

"That's okay. If we're alone, I'll probably cry. So let's just sit somewhere."

After we got our coffees I followed her to a couple of stools. The sky outside darkened dramatically. The latte was hot, and as I sipped it, I became increasingly anxious, not knowing how to broach the topic of my TPS file. It seemed wrong to bring it up.

"Tell me more about the flaky patient again?"

I had just clicked on with Sam, pressed the phone to my ear. I knew she was referring to the potential patient named Violet, but I hadn't revealed her name. "Oh, that gal has not really decided on using our clinic. I'm not even sure she's capable of getting back into fertility procedures. She calls Maple all the time and hassles her. I mean, most IVF patients are nervous, but I think this one's manic." Maple had described her once as a flooded toilet.

Since my meeting with Belle and now talking to Sam, I took in the foreboding sky that was too dark to be afternoon. Walking alone, I tucked my chin in and was thinking I might order Belle some flowers, but I couldn't remember what block my friend Eli had his shop on. When Sam asked another question about Violet, I answered. "No, she can't be a part of the sabotage. I don't think so."

Sam shocked me. "Could she be another actress in the play? Someone else perhaps Harrison was also messing around with?"

My fingers tightened around the phone. My heart thudded.

A play, an actress, lots of fairies.

"I can barely hear you," I said, my voice growing in decibel. "I doubt that. She has a husband. So no, a part of the embryo switch in the lab? It's implausible. She's manic but not like that."

"Sorry, but I'll have to try you later. I can't hear you either."

Wind raced like mad right at me, and I ducked below the eaves of an alley storefront. Other people had the same idea.

"It's a storm. Got to go."

"Okay, but there's still something else I've got—" The phone cut out.

I jostled loose and made it to the next storefront. The wind shuddered to a halt. Then ripped in another direction.

I slid the phone into my jacket pocket. A block later the huge rain pellets drenched me, and I had to seek cover. This time I was near the Corner Bakery. I yanked the door open.

I found a spot away from the window. People around me joked about the weather.

Watching the chaos, I caught my breath. Harrison had impregnated Janie, Sara, and who knows who else. Ben told me Harrison went to the DF lab a lot. Could he have gotten to Fanny?

Suddenly the planet began to shift.

Fanny could identify Harrison. She'd know which of the guys—Ben or Harrison—came to the clinic that particular day when I was in Houston.

Everyone distrusted her, though. Grateful she'd left our clinic. I had to bear in mind that she was currently working for them. She wouldn't jeopardize her new position at Dream Fertility, would she?

However, I could tell her there could be negligence on her part, too, for allowing them into the lab on a day, historical now, for embryo foul play.

What if she was now bedmates with Harrison and I never got to learn the truth?

The freezing rain had made its way through my coat, my shirt. The chills ran down my spine.

Thirty

I WAS WASTING time standing in the café. If all these questions lingered, dangled, and disrupted my life, I would be closer—no matter how you cut it—to finding answers for them at the lab.

That made sense to me.

Still the rain beat down, and I ducked into a cab with a brave driver—or maybe he was just opportunistic.

"Medical suite on Blackstone Avenue, thanks." I shouted to be heard over the wipers and the driving downpour. Janie and Beth texted to invite me to the movies. I shot them a quick reply that I was headed to the clinic.

I had to get out of these clothes; I could change into scrubs and wash them at home.

When we swerved from a wind gust, I couldn't help but notice that the cabbie tightened his grip on the steering wheel. Fortunately, no cars were coming in the opposing lane. Few cars were out. Debris marked the roadway.

I took the keys to the clinic out of my purse and held them in my fist while listening to the cadence of the rain. I'd counted to fifty-three when he interrupted. "Here you are lady."

"I'll double tip you for it, thank you. Stay dry."

The glass doors to the clinic were rain-streaked, and I fumbled with the keys. Finally inside, I dripped as I moved. Halfway to the elevator, my iTime vibrated, and I stopped under the atrium.

At last, it was Luke. But his eyes looked vacant. Something was wrong. "You must be exhausted."

"I'm not entirely sure what I am." Abrupt. "Why're you all soaked?"

"Weather's bad."

Luke looked back at me; he was wearing his typical high-powered investment banker suit, but his face was pale. He said, "I am not the same man, Julia."

I believed that if I had not been to the Dave Matthews concert in the fall with Beth at Tinley Park, I wouldn't be having this moment now. Yet, thrilled as I was he'd iTimed me, I couldn't help but feel it might come crashing down. When love provides fireworks, it's not realistic to believe the vivid colors and tantalizing pops can remain airborne.

"I just need some time," he said. "I guess."

"What kind of time?" Luna had suggested this. Holding back hysterics, I said, "I talked to your mom."

"Did she tell you?"

This all didn't seem like normal behavior. "Yes. You know where the emeralds are so you'll make another trip down there."

"And what else did she tell you?" Worry.

"Just . . . that you decided to go after them." My voice choked out.

"No, that's not it. We are half—" he looked away. Back again.

iTime didn't lag; the delay was all him.

"Halfway what?" I turned angry. "You're not all the way in love with me. Is that what you're too cowardly to say?"

"I can't say it."

My heart was shaking like a leaf. I forced it out. "You're not in love with me."

"I can't be." He looked broken. "There are some fierce reasons why it might not work out."

"Fierce reasons? What are you talking about? Who cares about an emerald mine?"

"Julia"—he gave me a long stare—"You don't know what you're saying."

The planet turned upside down.

My heart ached, and never having seen this side of him, I vowed to be there for him all the more. "I'm so sorry the emeralds have you stressed. Sorry too about your ETF, that it's not working out like you thought, but we have to try."

"Look, I have to go." His gaze turned downward, like to his wrist, and his shoulder moved too.

No, don't press that button. "Don't—"

He did. I had to call him back. I had every intention of doing that.

Some pregnant lady started banging on the front door.

It was Janie. She should be at home.

I ran to the door and yanked it open. The storm reached a crescendo, and I got goose bumps seeing how wet she was and looking into her eager eyes.

"Come in," I said. "My God, I know you wanted to see a film, but what are you doing out in this?"

First thing, she begged to use the bathroom. So we went to the nearest one in the lobby, and by that point she was hunched over. The door was locked.

I didn't know where Maple kept the key.

We raced to the elevator and made it to the fourth floor, where I sent her to the restroom. I found some warm clothes for her and left them outside the door.

Finally, I went to my office to change too. While there I recalled an idea about our lab workstations, and I remembered David and

I had brainstormed upgrading to more of a team-based laboratory space. Beyond the team, I had the thought of technology robots, and the ability to automate and speak with innovators on this. But sneaking into my thoughts was Sam, her saying that there was something else. I wondered if it was about Harrison? My biggest concern was his personal motivation in all this. Did it relate back to his religious beliefs like Sam suggested?

I closed the blinds, thinking it would block out the sound of the wind and help me concentrate. On a website I quickly located the guidelines for Catholics who were facing infertility. I read about how Catholics in this dilemma can actually get tested for reproductive ailments. But others, and they are significant, are considered morally wrong. This stated that they were going against the Church if there was any procedure performed that was an alternative for marital intercourse. Where this mainly applied was semen samples obtained through masturbation. So artificial insemination with sperm from a donor was obviously right in line with that, and therefore not permissible.

So what? Could someone really be against this?

Janie entered, and I brought up the subject. "Why did you come? Are you okay?"

When she just smiled at me, I said, "I never knew all this about Catholicism and infertility."

She stared back, dumbfounded. "What's that have to do with the price that babies cost these days?" She laughed. "I mean tea in China."

Her spirits didn't seem rocked. "You did get my message about Harrison?"

"Oh, he's the devil in a surfer's body," she said. "And I wanted to tell you in person, it's okay."

I laughed. "Glad you see it that way. But I can't believe you came here in a storm carrying a baby in there."

"You have always been there for me."

"Well, thank you." I went around and wrapped my arms around her. I felt similar electricity in the moment as when I clasped Belle at the coffee shop. "If you're up for it, I can fill you in a bit on Harrison."

She nodded theatrically, big eyes and eyebrows arched, and she leaned forward.

"Harrison and his brother were raised in California, by Gene and Olive, and they taught their boys to obey the moral Catholic law."

"You probably don't treat a lot of Catholics."

"We don't discuss religion." Again I pondered Harrison's vendetta and stance on this and babies. Clearly, he wasn't afraid to procreate himself. Maybe he *only* wanted to procreate. I dismissed it. "Nobody's that naïve. Earlier I had a flashback to a James Bond movie that my dad and I watched a long time ago. The villain was all for creating only the ultimate human species, in which everyone was athletic, cunning, and lithe—and brainwashed!"

Janie didn't laugh. She stared at me.

"Let me take you there," she said.

I smelled sodden, a bit like wet asphalt from the rain, and I was not itching to go back outside. "Where?"

"Here," and I watched her point at her lustrous, dark hair, made more shiny by pregnancy hormones.

"Your mind?" I said incredulously.

"Yes, close your eyes." She cocked her head. The smile ran away. "I'm not kidding."

With the blinds already drawn, there was very little light in the room. I closed my eyes and squeezed out the rest.

"You've been to the Shakespeare Theatre, to see my performance of *A Midsummer Night's Dream*." Her voice dripped like honey. "I have nothing against people with stout religious beliefs. But, here goes, I'm describing the scene. I'm taking you to my dress rehearsal."

Solemn now, an odd reflex had me lacing my hands together in prayer.

"Overhead the heat fixture is humming, and I'm excited to see

Harrison, actually I'm zinging like a horse in heat, and I really can't wait to practice onstage with him, and race off to my place afterwards.

"I'm inside the theater. Taking the stage. But why? There's no one here. Where's the cast? How long do I wait? My mind objects, and I get mad at myself for being wrong about rehearsal time.

"I lift my chin and my ears prick.

"Footsteps.

"I pause but then I ease to the side of the stage, in a wing. Hidden from view.

"A real-time heartbeat, mine. It's so loud. I think I'll be discovered.

"A musty swell. I reach for the heavy curtain and pull it over me. Except I need to see.

"One man's voice only.

"I breathe quietly.

"I'm afraid.

"He's talking gibberish. Muttering things.

"Before I could raise the curtain and go to Harrison, I see his belt's undone.

"A lump rises in my throat."

I swallowed hard, breathing deeply. I'm still holding my eyes closed.

"I rise to my feet.

"A sound. Loud. He's knocked into several seats.

"And a groan.

"My heavens!

"Some other person must be with him.

"My chest heaves.

"He begins to take his pants down.

"My gut tells me someone else is coming, but there's no one. He's saying 'Sara, Janie, Margaret, Mary, take me. My sweet babies,' and he's grinding on himself so furiously and he's groaning and calling out, and it's all a blend of names. Mine's in there, for God's sake.

'Forgive me. I don't care, Father. I don't care anymore,' he lets loose."

My fingertips have dug in so hard. I opened my eyes. Horizontal indentations run along the tops of my hands. I looked around and found Janie.

Tears crested her cheekbones.

I tried over and over to get up. Then I rose and hugged my friend.

Thirty One

I DON'T KNOW how long Janie waited behind the curtain.

I didn't ask. I did keep religion and faith and fertility in mind two days later when giving the press conference with Belle and Tanya and their husbands Theo and Boyd. I was still astonished by what info Ben had found in Sara's office.

Since last week we'd hired a law firm to investigate the evidence, which Ben shared with them, too: travel manifests, threatening email, evidence of a possible break-in at our California clinic. He'd been able to say he wasn't at the Chicago lab the actual day of the mix-up, but couldn't provide a substantiated alibi. That was a problem and left Fanny holding the cards, and . . . she wouldn't call me back.

The media calls flooded in and were mostly favorable. I had a quick conversation with Tia, Susanna, Daryl, Demetri and the rest of the staff to discuss what to say if approached by the media; we decided consistency was key. We weren't necessarily cleared of liability, but the world was feeling empathetic with regards to the mix-up of embryos. Even more so toward Belle and Theo.

David and I refused to allow an interview in the lab room. It halted lab work, so I told reporters we would convene in our conference room. There were so many of us, and in fact we didn't want so many people in the lab or perfumes or scents that could affect the embryos.

David sat to my right around the table. We had a counselor in with us, a nurse, and the IVF doctor, Pete Dandridge, who'd handled the IVF.

I took in the expressions of the patients.

Theo was wearing a pensive look that reminded me of Luke. I actually teared up and had to pretend to turn off my phone. The memories triggered were so powerful. I blinked away the welling tears.

Boyd, loud and joking, exuded hints of tobacco.

Tanya, sweet, like a flower, reminded me of magnolias.

I noticed Tanya being attentive to Belle, who of course smelled like baby lotion, a salve on the tight mound of her abdomen, an itch reliever.

For twenty minutes the conversation centered on how the people felt badly for these two couples and what the ramifications were for improved security and quality control in the lab and clinical settings.

David and I took turns with questions on the latter.

Reporter Charles for KBY News seemed satisfied with our answers.

He addressed Dr. Dandridge. "How do you feel about the possibility that you may have been infiltrated by outside embryologists?"

"It's immoral. It's an outright act against science and progress and human rights."

Charles nodded. "I'd presume that you'd need to have personal faith to go through these infertility procedures." He was stating to the general group, but all eyes turned to Belle at the same instant.

"I am in agreement with that," she said. "However, I do feel like one's style and beliefs are what keep all IVF patients in different universes. What I desire and want to achieve is unlike others. I still refuse to adopt. I'm still upset about IVF, and I remain"—her nostrils flared—"against Theo and me using donor eggs."

I looked at my iTime; Susanna and Tia had scheduled embryo grading. I said, "Thank you." I smiled and clapped my hands gently. "That's a wrap."

After all this, we still didn't know how to make Belle happy.

By Wednesday I was working out twice a day and, when not exer-cising, arming myself with coffee. After an afternoon yoga class, I walked briskly down the street, returning with a mega latte for me as well as one for Maple.

She thanked me and said, "Sorry to tell you—Fanny McCloud is on her way."

We heard the break between doors, a puff of air. Fanny stood there, paused, tossing a black scarf across her shoulder. One side of her blonde hair swept back and folded in with it. Then she saw us.

I flinched. Here we go.

I felt the meeting warranted a private setting, so I led her beyond the atrium to an unoccupied patient room. After I closed the door, we stared at one another in silence.

"Remember how you said to me, you will regret this?" Fanny's hands closed around both hips. "Well, I do regret leaving your clinic. By the water cooler at DF, some people have been sniggering."

"Who?"

"You met her—Sara Lance, the supervisor."

I nodded, watching her eyes.

"I eavesdropped. Something seemed wrong. Both Harrison and Ben were always around. Their laughing made me wonder because there was an edge to it; it seemed all wrong," she said again. "You know, callous."

Yeah, you would know, I thought, but backed down. She was trying to tell me something.

"Sara said, 'Great plan to come up with the Embryo Clinic. They think they're geniuses—well, they fell for it.'" Fanny took a deep breath. "And the guy was saying 'I just wish our success rates and our staff could get it right. Be as good as theirs. One day we will be superior.'"

Just then I recalled how the day they were in my lab asking for data. I could've cut the air with a knife. But my mind was temporarily derailed. Fanny, of all people, was reporting on jealousy. "And you? What's your motivation for telling me this about Dream Fertility and Harrison?" I had a dry mouth.

Her hands went to her hips. She brushed her hair from her blue eyes, impenetrable as granite. "Difference between right and wrong. I've quit so many clinics; I'll never get a job this time. It doesn't matter. But the people who come to Advanced Fertility National to get treatment? They matter."

I described Janie's situation, but kept most of the drama out of it. Fanny listened quietly.

"Harrison's motives are unclear to me," I said, "but he must think those men who give samples get off with a freedom he doesn't have. It's strange. Why else?"

Not a peep. Not a laugh.

"I don't know," I answered myself. "It sounds like a personal problem."

She pinched her hands harder into her waist. "It was Ben. By the cooler that day."

I gasped. Was Ben framing Harrison?

"Also, I saw *his* tickets. Ben was in California at the same time."

Then I couldn't be sure one way or the other. I shivered.

She upturned her palms. "The mix-up? It was definitely Ben at CLB that day."

When it was time to leave, I wobbled out the front door of the clinic. "The investigation is going to get crazy now." To my own ears, my voice sounded a million miles away.

My fingers let go of the door handle and slid down into my pocket, seeking warmth. I'd forgotten gloves.

I dragged myself to the cabstand. The ground was slick, and I watched my footsteps so I didn't slip. I heard traffic. Lavender dusk was forming in the sky.

Life is about finding someone, I thought. And I'm no closer than I ever was. My finger slid along a sharp edge, deep down in my pocket. A paper cut. It burned. I yanked out the culprit and then stared at the ticket to the Ledge, exactly 1,353 feet above the street. The Ledge began calling my name.

That's when I tried to take off the iTime again. The clasp wouldn't budge. I lifted my head, let out a huge breath, and then sank back into myself to wait my turn for a cab.

When I made it to the front of the line at the Willis Tower, I asked if the ticket was still useable for the Skydeck. I didn't know if there was an expiration date for it. Frankly, did I really care if I walked out onto the see-through space and fainted?

I actually smiled when the attendant punched the ticket and waved me on. He closed the red rope behind me. It made me think of Meaghan's Twizzlers.

Up to the Ledge I was going, to hammer it out, let my emotions free fall to an endless street. I was going by myself. Being alone was my only way out.

Then Jason cut through the crowd.

I had to steel my heart.

"I have a ticket," he said. "You don't believe me?"

"Be careful." I managed a smile. "I cut myself on it." I held up my finger as proof. Blood had seeped all around the cuticle.

"Let me get you a tissue."

I waved a hand but he turned and got one somewhere quickly.

When he returned, I said bitterly, "Besides, I'm not with Luke anymore so you don't need to follow or protect me."

I dabbed at the cut.

His eyes were clouding. "I'm sorry about Luke."

"Word travels fast." I battled emotions.

We stepped forward in the line, the waiting almost over. I allowed him to hold my hand. I felt nothing but nervousness about walking onto the Skydeck Ledge. I couldn't believe I could still feel this bothered by the sheer act of walking out onto the glass floor. I'd just been dumped. That was much worse.

And there was Jason. He'd probably sky-dived the world over to protect this person or that landing zone. He calmly took off his sunglasses.

My heart quivered. I had wet palms, but I didn't care.

I ignored the Ledge photographer too.

Looking straight out, my focus on the horizon did not falter. I refused to look down. I knew the Ledge was cantilevered.

British visitors were loud in front of us, talking about the three layers of half-inch glass for the floor of the balcony.

That's all? As far as I was concerned it was the most terrifying viewing platform of all time. I'd rather have been in a glass tank surrounded by sharks. I'd rather have had nineteen hundred paper cuts. I'd rather have been stuck in an emerald mine.

My ethos could change in a matter of minutes. I clenched my fists. If I could overcome this, I could move forward in a mind-body balance again. I knew it.

My body moved forward.

I, Julia Holland, was standing on the Ledge.

The next afternoon I performed a trophectoderm biopsy on a blastocyst embryo, which involved removing a few cells to send to a genetics lab for chromosomal testing. In walked a double surprise. Swan and Sam stood in the doorway.

"Hello," they said in unison.

I tugged off the rubber gloves, but stayed seated.

Sam looked argumentative. "You haven't called either of us back. We were trying to tell you we want to help you."

"So you came here?" Half of me was charged with curiosity by the unplanned visit; the other half felt annoyed. "I was trying to, but—can we change the subject?"

"Sure." She rolled her shoulders back. They came in and stood near me. "We took a flight because it's really important, and it has to do with you. Because in my new position, we uncovered something. Your real biological mother was from our NYC clinic."

I rolled the chair back. "I beg your pardon?"

"Through Dr. Swan, I know that your mother's ultrasound was time stamped." She paused. "It matches the signature look of others from that period of time."

"This isn't true. Why did you tell her this?"

Swan deferred to Sam.

"I work there. Don't look so surprised. You gave him my number, remember? He hired me."

"Yes, okay, now go back." I didn't really believe what she was spinning. "What're you saying? Other clinics could use similar timestamps."

"Ask your mother. Find out the donor clinic."

"I don't need to. She went to a Miami clinic." Either the ultrasound was wrong or Sam was. "Do you hear yourself? Ridiculous. How're you able to divulge this anyway? Donor info is confidential."

Swan raised his hand to his forehead, massaged it. He looked directly at me. His voice was low. "In certain situations, yes. But your mother signed a form that allows for you to find out when you're eighteen, *plus*, it's a roadblock-type situation. There is a blood relationship issue."

"What do you mean?"

"My email was not about Tanya's twins. It was meant for you."

"Go on." I looked to Sam.

"Your biological donor was Luna Ashton."

Thirty Two

"IMPOSSIBLE." IT WAS really not possible. My feet were like lead. I blinked again and again. Life ground to a halt.

From the leather portfolio in his lap, Swan withdrew the ultrasound image. He flipped it over and showed me the proof for real. Faint, but legible, the timestamp showing the letters NYEC.

That's when I grabbed my stomach and took several deep breaths. In what seemed like forever, I whispered, "She can't be."

Sam interrupted me. "She is. You left the image in New York. He just knew"—she pointed to Swan—"and pieced it together. Your mannerisms are just like Luna's. He says they match. And she donated eggs after having the second son, after the friend's accident. You've known her for thirty years, right?"

Swan gazed toward me solemnly and tilted his head. "I'm sorry."

The news about my hidden identity stayed out of the public eye for a little while. Beth and her family invited me to Amelie's Spelling Bee and over for every Taco Tuesday night. The distractions were welcome. Beth even made me a fountain in the shape of a starfish. I found a special spot for it in the kitchen.

Later that night I started to feel low. I couldn't help but wonder where I saw myself in twenty years. Still fretting over the fact I fell in love with my half-brother?

The 600-person twin study had ambiguous findings. We were not twins, but we found out we were blood related—after the fact. How did I feel about the stunning revelation? How did I feel that we made love? That he touched me all over. And why didn't I have some built-in instinct that it was wrong?

And my favorite memory: When he cocked his head, the light caught the vertical indentation, centered in his chin.

I took a long bath and felt a little calmer, until Sam called and tried to get me to talk.

"Leave me alone for a little while," I said. "Do you mind?"

"No way. Stop sulking."

"I'm not sulking! I'm busy."

"Listen, Racy, I know it will all work out."

She's incorrigible. "I hope so."

David and I talked it over. We called Swan. The three of us decided we might share my history with the media so it wouldn't be discovered later and get sensationalized. I found myself headlining in the current newspaper in two places: one covered the half-truth about the iTime swimsuit modeling and the other detailed the whole truth about my identity. The Internet had photos of me, mostly going in or leaving the clinic, but there was also one at the Ledge with Jason. It was pretty disturbing. I scanned the captions; some were cruel like "Embryologist Stirs It Up With Brother and Friend." At least word wasn't out Jason was Luke's bodyguard and employee.

Did Luna know? Had Swan talked to her?

What about Luke? Was there really an emerald heist or was it the means in which he could extricate himself from the relationship? How do you kill the love?

Everyone seemed paralyzed by the blood relationship.

Where was I donor-conceived? Miami or New York?

Why didn't the journalists make it all one story?

I needed to get out, get some fresh air, but it was ten p.m. I was turning nocturnal.

The phone rang. It logged Belle Harting as the caller.

I picked up.

"Sorry it's late, Julia. Are you okay?"

"Sort of." I didn't feel I sounded convincing.

"I have been feeling so sorry for myself but when I learned of you, I decided my situation wasn't so awful. It's human nature to think you're the only one hurting. Especially for infertile women!"

"Hey, I've heard that before." Everyone I'd ever worked with in IVF seemed like an island. "I thought maybe you called to ask me to coffee again, but it's a little late for that. Go on, tell me how the twins are doing."

"No."

"Pardon me?"

"This is about you."

Oh come on. It was like, the new line for everybody.

"I used to run marathons. Tanya was addicted to making partner in the law firm. Fertility problems for both of us."

This gave me pause. Another reason I wanted to create Hiatus was to develop some research on the implications of stress related to excessive exercise and overworking. How it all related. I knew there were implications, but how much?

"I know." I didn't sound like a puppet anymore, because against my will, purpose was forming. "Your current situation is epic. Let's talk about this; maybe we should just do it over coffee tomorrow."

"Sure, Julia—anything. Anything for you."

I found myself back at the coffee place Pierrot Gourmet the next day. After we began to sip our hot beverages, Belle said there was something she wanted to show me.

I walked by her side several blocks to the Rhythm and Blues Museum. The entrance was light and airy. There was an atrium made of dark barn wood.

"It was very cold outside when I was here last. Twenty below or something. I remember I just had to come, and then when I was viewing legendary guitars of the musicians who created this musical phenomenon, I had this premonition. I would have a girl. I placed my hand here"—she laughed—"but I was ripped back then."

We found an open bench.

I recalled Belle's obsession with TRX classes. Whenever I'd done it, I was so sore I couldn't convince myself to go back before a month had passed.

"But I felt pregnant. I just knew."

It felt like a moment I might remember forever. We sat on the bench in the long hall and a couple of times I gazed up to look at the ceilings stretching high above. I felt angels could be surrounding us. Invisible yet present, and I thought of a powerful trident and music playing on a harp, plus rhythm and blues, Greek mythology, alas my own spirituality. At the same instant I was calm and floored by the power of intuition Belle was sharing.

"I know you like music so I thought you'd appreciate it here."

Before I could go into her options, she said, "This is such an amazing place." She rotated her gaze 180 degrees back toward me. "You are why I even considered this notion of Tanya's. It's your philosophy of hope. Through IVF and any other option available. And how women who want a career and family shouldn't settle for the high percentage of infertility among women in their early thirties."

She'd reached a crescendo. "Like me. Thank you. Thank you so much for bringing me hope."

"What does this mean?"

"You had faith in me while I doubted everything. You never gave up. Right now, all my energy goes into this pregnancy. Theo and I plan to adopt—" she began to pat her belly, "one of these."

Then she laced her fingers atop of the twins.

I wasn't expecting more.

"There's someone who wanted me to set up a meeting with you. We met in the hallway at the clinic, a while back."

"Who?" Footsteps followed.

"Hi," he said.

"Luke."

As best she could, Belle slipped out. She forgot her purse and by the time she came back for it, Luke and I still had not spoken.

"I'm just glad you didn't fall for Harrison. You could have a baby on the way."

"Could be worse. *We* could have a baby on the way."

Neither of us laughed at the joke.

"I will miss all that." He spoke gently.

I knew what he meant.

He cleared his throat. "It's possible to erase and start over, I guess." He studied his iTime watch, and then said, "Jason said the iTime was stuck on you."

I managed a smile. "Bad irony, huh?"

"When you want to take it off there's an automatic release app."

"Why didn't I think of that?"

"It's here." He leaned over and scrolled to a screen, then showed me the icon. He pressed the button for me. I smelled how good and clean he smelled, and it about drove me crazy. I rolled my eyes to myself.

"Don't want me to get gooey. So . . . I'll be around." He pulled a ticket from his pocket. "I have a chance to use these." Two tickets.

For a long minute, I saw a glimmer in his eyes. "You can take Beth or Janie."

I thought they were Skydeck tickets.

His laugh erupted. "Julia Holland is by far the best person to go with to see the Dave Matthews Band. Would you agree?"

"Yes, Luke." My mouth gaped. "Concert tickets, wow! Thank you."

Thirty Three

HOW MANY TIMES in life do you say—this is better because we are doing it together?

There was Sam, who just wouldn't let it go. And for that I will be forever grateful. Friendship is threaded, the thickness like roots that spread and interlock. Let me tell you the rest.

I was standing in line at a health food store, wearing my black workout tights, soft shell jacket, and hot pink Adidas, when I heard the sound of my inbox growing. After I was rung up and paid for the quinoa salad, coconut water, and pistachio ice cream, I checked my phone. Beth had emailed with confirmation numbers for our flights to Florida. "I'm taking you back home so you can do some thinking."

Five days later, I'd rearranged my life so the three of us could go. Tucker would tag along too. The day of travel to Key Largo was uneventful, though my nerves were all tricked out again. I was going to see my parents and hear the God's honest truth straight from my mother.

We were unlocking the door to the cottage adjacent to my parent's villa when I said, "I wish Janie could've come." Her doctor wanted her on bed rest, and from there she could do admin work for the theater. "I love that she still wants to name the baby Pier."

That afternoon before dinner at my parents', Tucker and I made a list of names for Belle and Tanya's twins. Apalachicola (he found it on my phone by googling Trip Advisor), and, of course, "Gator" was mixed in. He smiled at me. "A double name? Anne Gator."

I shrugged. "Why not?" I passed him his visor to Velcro to his backpack.

We were heading out early the next morning to hit some balls on the clay court in the Cay Harbor development, though I noticed swollen clouds heading our way.

We left the cottage with Beth. After securing our drinks in the cup holders, we drove the rented golf cart to the store for a few extra limes and a flower arrangement for my mom.

On our way back I turned to Tucker. "You know, Gator is a pretty crazy name."

"It's perfect."

Then Tucker caught me rolling my eyes.

"I don't roll my eyes at people anymore. You know why? I tried it out and it really hurts."

He had a point. The wind blew back his hair. His white smile gleamed in the near-dark.

After a casual seafood dinner and a bottle of wine, I walked Beth out to the front porch. Tucker ran back for his iPad and then joined us. The night sky had turned milky white with a navy haze behind it. The clouds smelled tropical and rich, salty almost.

I kissed Tucker goodnight. "I'll be along shortly."

Back up at the screened-in porch, my mom was removing all the pillows on the wicker furniture, except for the love seat. When she sat, I joined her.

"Honey, I'm feeling guilty. I haven't been honest with you."

"Why?" I flipped my hair out of my eyes. My adrenaline kicked up a notch. "The donor clinic wasn't here?"

Silence.

I tried to respond in a nice tone, but I couldn't. "You always said it was—"

"I never said it was here; you assumed it. It's in New York, the same clinic you merged with. I was afraid you'd find out your biological mother—"

I set the dessert plate down hard on the wicker table standing between us. It rattled, and the chocolate cake flipped sideways. I couldn't eat it.

"And want to have a life with her."

I was still thinking about me. They all had a chance: Luna, Luke, and Mom, but they couldn't. Did they think it would change my whole life, career and all, or make me stop loving them?

I groaned. And all of a sudden my face grew hot, because I'd been pent up about this. "Why didn't you want me to find the donor mother?"

"It's not the only reason. I already felt like I'd finagled you into the world. After the accident I didn't want you to have an even more complicated life."

"What accident are you talking about?" I'd never heard anything of this sort before.

Hmm.

The horror of the Ledge wasn't an imagined fear. My mom had dropped me from a fishing bridge. My infant body had plummeted from Seven Mile Bridge on US 1. I fell over sixty feet into the sea. Either the warmth of the water or buoyancy of babies or the resiliency of a three-month-old gave me a second chance.

My father had been fishing for yellowtail underneath that spot on the bridge; my mother had taken me up to see him from above. She'd protected my vanilla skin with sunscreen, which facilitated my slipping from her hands. He retrieved me from the water and bundled me in towels. Good magic? Destiny? A lucky break? Whichever one you chose.

My parents had been terrified of losing me. They went directly to the hospital, had me checked over, every inch. End of the story: the thought of losing me to anyone, especially at eighteen when I knew of my donor-conception, bound them to a mutual pledge. I wasn't going to be shared with another person, even if she was the donor.

My entanglement with heights rang true.

My recent merger with *the* clinic in New York brought a twinge of guilt to both of them, but the life's journey with me to this point forged a stronger bond. Made their will even more resilient. But that didn't help me.

On the porch at her home, my mom's tears fell. She wept. "I feel the burden of guilt," she said. She sniffed and waggled a finger in the air. "But now, if you aren't going to kill me, I can let go of my fear."

"Mom, you won't lose me."

The following morning I tore off the 3 for April. I dropped it on the counter so Dad could read the Far Side comic.

At two a.m. I'd heard a child's scream, followed by a thunder boomer. Then Beth's voice as she went to him. It took me a while to fall back to sleep. They were still snoozing.

After Beth left for Chicago, I headed into the kitchen before going on some runs. There was a bag on the white tile counter. I opened the envelope at the top and inhaled the thick aroma of dark Colombian coffee. I set it to the far back of the pantry and grabbed two small containers instead. The Keurig began to froth the vanilla latte part. It spit the last bit in.

I piled on the thoughts. Belle had unexplained infertility, some said from too much running.

Tanya worked excessively.

It further upset the apple cart when Ben switched the embryos. Still, two took.

Twins being born in July.

Ben was for himself.

He was against advancement.

He was his own establishment, and he convinced Sara to see it his way.

She met Harrison, thinking he was fun to watch perform.

She discovered he was troubled from youth, fraying from the Catholicism rope.

Harrison equaled easy prey.

They would frame him.

But something went wrong. Remorse, arousal, both?

A baby conceived for Sara.

Ben tried to get even with her by giving me partial evidence.

Somewhere near the same time: *A Midsummer Night's Dream.*

My actress friend falls for actor.

Janie's baby, she wanted to call Pier.

My uncertainty with two mothers. *What do I call Luna?* Or not at all.

Who is Luke Ashton really?

Navy Pier had fireworks.

Fertility and fireworks.

Black coffee, step two, ran smoothly onto the milky bottom. Steam rose.

A few minutes later I was on the sofa, with a book open on my lap, when the call came in. The one I'd been dreading. From so-and-so, the iTime brand manager. I couldn't even remember his name.

"I'm sorry, I'm in Key Largo, not planning to be back in Chicago for thirty days."

"It's all right. We can work with that. How about down there? You can't beat that for an intoxicating and paradise-like setting."

I considered that. I couldn't freak out anymore. "That's just fine."

So the next morning when the white Chevy Tahoe showed up I was standing in the front yard of the little rental cottage beside my parents' bigger home, where the last of the branches remained from last night's storm. The air was thick, tepid. I was cleaning up debris. I heard the clap as the door opened. It wasn't the photographer. When Jason's muscular frame emerged, I gasped for a breath. He looked sharp in a pressed shirt with dark jeans. I took a few steps forward, barefoot in the spongy wet grass.

He came over but stopped short. "How are you?"

"The gate guard let you by? Friends have to be called in."

"I'm a friend?"

I ignored his attempt at witticism. "You heard about the ultrasound that traces me to Luna Ashton? Two colleagues, one is my best friend, discovered it."

"Are you sure they can be trusted?"

I laughed. "Want me to show you the ultrasound?"

"No, not if it's that old. It's probably as grainy as the first satellite images we used to take of the landing zones. You couldn't tell anything. Something that looked like a benign log was really a sniper or two."

He went on, "Jules, for your knowledge I've talked to the investigating officers on Advanced Fertility's case to book Sara and Ben on extortion, too. Basically they've been fudging the amount on the patients' billing. Also, I told Maple that I found out more about Ben. He covered up a stint in his past he didn't like. He played baseball in college, used steroids to beef up, be a better athlete. When he was on top, there was a pop quiz.

"Drug testing. He didn't pass, because he was using steroids. After I learned that I went to his Lake Forest home. No one was there so I took the liberty of letting myself in, and guess what I uncovered? A rather large heroin stash. He's a lifetime junkie." Jason's eyes shifted. "No wonder their stats aren't that great. You can't operate like that."

"How do you know all this again?" I felt the morning chill and tightened the wrap sweater against my chest.

"I'm in the security business."

Don-don-don-dah. I said, "Right on." Nervous, I had the weird impulse to reach for him. I crossed my arms. "There's a pattern of you following me around the country, and it's getting a little—"

"Uncomfortable?"

I was going with hair-raising. There ensued silence.

"I like you."

"What? That night, when I—" What should I say? "You acted like I was the only one in the room. Besides, I want someone else." I lied.

His charcoal eyes softened, which was a bit out of character for him, and I couldn't look away. I thought about the interest he'd taken in the Advanced Fertility investigation.

"When you make a living in security, you have a contract to uphold. It's like you. Whatever it takes for your patients. It's all I have. Had." He waited. "I've changed that for you. I don't work for anyone."

"You're not making sense." I didn't feel like trying, or rather, I realized I was exhausted.

"Listen, I'm in my thirties. Do you know I worry about the biological clock ticking, and how to balance that with my career and a life partner? Even though men can sire children late into their seventies, I don't want to be that person! I don't want to postpone fatherhood too late into life. I want to participate fully in my kid's life."

This confession. Would he ever have had the strength to tell me his feelings if I hadn't found out that Luke was my half-brother? "I thought you were a career bodyguard."

"I have more to offer." He reached for my face.

I moved out of the way. But my breath caught at the same time. My dreaming heart perched on a ledge.

We discussed Luke. "I forgot to ask him. The emeralds were really stolen?"

He nodded. "Luke wanted me to tell you 'I 2 u.'"

My fists clenched. He noticed.

"Thanks." My hands loosened; they were shaking now because I wanted to touch him. "It would mean a lot to me if you could be around Chicago when the twins are born."

"When is the due date?"

My eyes never lost touch. "Twins generally come early. I'm estimating the Fourth of July."

Happy explosion. I was swerving toward Jason.

He caught me. "I like what's happening here."

At the same time the door to the cottage shot open.

"What's going on, Ju-Ju? Hey." Tucker pointed at Jason while scrunching his nose. "I remember you. Where's Heath? Did you bring him too?"

By this time we'd separated and the little guy was up to us in the yard.

"It's okay, Tucker. Maybe we could Skype him." I let go. "Are you sticking around for dinner, Jason?"

Pause. "Yes. Think I will." He grabbed a handful with a branch and wet leaves and went to empty it into the black sack by the sidewalk. We watched him.

"What's he really here for?" Tucker asked when Jason had gone to gather other tree limbs near a row of towering bougainvillea.

I leaned over. "Little guy, the bad guys are going to pay for what they did to my patients."

He smiled with enthusiasm. "That's good. Bad guys keep me up at night."

Acknowledgments

To Virginia Frankel, for going on the trips to see Dave Matthews Band in Chicago and Salt Lake!

To Jen DiStefano, for being a content guru, and now friend.

To Tim Sandlin, Tina Welling, Shawn Klomparens, and Cathie Pelletier, for making writing a gorgeous art.

To Jamie Poff for lifting my writing up, at a formidable age.

To Brenda Wylie, Andrea Loban, Alex Maher, Sarah Kilmain, Jennie Vogel, and Lydia Hudacsko for being my first readers.

To Hannah Jones and Erica Dahlin, who took care of my babies while I worked on this.

To Tanya Hall, for taking a chance.

To Justin Branch, and everyone at Greenleaf Book Group, for all the intense labor.

To Rachael Brandenburg, for capturing the hope of fertility patients on the cover.

To Scott James, for making me feel one-of-a-kind.

To April Murphy, for managing the editorial process, *Kristine Peyre-Ferry and Brittany Lewis* who are leading the charge.

To Linda and Jay, for all your hard work and having the knack to be fun in the world of copyediting. You are masters of building rich stories and managing prose.

To Ashley Matthews, Dana Smith, Ellen Haag, Betsy Mollinet, Darcey Prichard, Scottie Pavlick, Meredith Adams, Tracy Poduska and Molly Hirshfield, for being such cool friends.

To Emilie Lyons, for your patience and faith.

To OB doctors and Fertility Specialists: Dr. Maura Lofaro, Dr. Shannon Roberts, Dr. Deb Minjarez, Dr. Eric Surrey and Dr. William Schoolcraft. Without you, we would be missing some of the greatest beings of all time.

To Lanie Love, for being a connector.

To embryologists out there, thank you.

To Evelyn Shura and Irmgard Salten, for knowing I could do it.

To Roy C. Kinsey III and IV and Asheley Carrington Kinsey, for being there for me.

To the Mahers, for unconditional love; writers are introverts, and you make living large look easy. *To Alex* especially . . .

And to my new readers: welcome to Julia Holland.